Th
Fan
men
—ha usiastic followers than astronomer Svir Hedrigs. So when Hedrigs learned that the only complete set of *Fantaisie* in existence had been bought by the tyrant Tar Benesh—for destruction, to demonstrate his wealth—he was ready to follow the mysterious Tatja Grimm in her plan to stop Benesh.

The trouble was, Tatja had some further plans—for Benesh, for Hedrigs, and for the whole planet.

GRIMM'S WORLD

VERNOR VINGE

Hamlyn Paperbacks

GRIMM'S WORLD

ISBN 0 600 34083 x

First published in Great Britain 1978 by
Hamlyn Paperbacks

Hamlyn Paperbacks are published by
The Hamlyn Publishing Group Ltd
Astronaut House,
Feltham,
Middlesex, England

Made and printed in Great Britain by
Cox & Wyman Ltd, London, Reading and Fakenham

PART I

CHAPTER 1

The tavern was old, luxurious—even respectable. Its sloping dance floor and high ceiling created the illusion that the hall was an open amphitheater. Crystal spheres cast an even, unwavering twilight over tables and patrons. Svir Hedrigs squinted gloomily at the newly polished table surface. Barely visible under the varnish were three centuries of minor vandalism. Krirsarque had been a university city for almost ten generations, and during that time, unnumbered students had carved their names in the durable furniture of the Bayside Arbor.

It was still early and not a third of the tables were occupied. The jongleurs were up on their platform, playing songs and doing acrobatics. So far their amusements had not drawn a single couple onto the dance floor. Svir grunted his disgust, and extended long knobby legs under the table. He absently caressed the furry body of the creature sitting on the table. The animal turned its outsize head toward him and regarded the man with limpid black eyes. A deep purring sound came from its wide, pointed ears. Then it turned away and scanned the hall, its tall ears flicking this way and that. Far across the hall, a waiter looked severely in their direction, began walking toward them. When he got to within three tables of Svir, he stopped, puzzled, with the air of someone who has forgotten his purpose. The waiter shook his head confusedly and headed back to the bar.

"Good boy Ancho," murmured Svir. Tonight he didn't want to argue with anyone about his pet's presence in the tavern. He had come out for one last fling before sailing tomorrow. Fling—hah! He knew he would just sit lumpishly till closing time. For the thousandth time he cursed his bad luck. Who'd have thought that his thesis topic would require him to sail all the way to Crownesse? Because of the season, that was more than ten days sailing time, unless one could afford hydrofoil passage—which he certainly could not.

The hall was filling now, but as he surveyed it, Svir concluded with sick self-pity that this night he didn't have the courage to tour the tables, importuning unattached girls. He slouched back and made a determined effort to finish his drink in one draft.

"May I join you?" The soft voice came from behind and above. Svir choked violently on his *skaal*, spewing the liquid in all directions. His fit of choking gave him a chance to see that the speaker was as pretty as her voice.

"Please do!" he gasped painfully, trying to regain some shred of poise. "Miss, uh . . . ?"

"Tatja Grimm." The miracle lowered herself gracefully into the chair next to his, and set her drink on the table next to Ancho's right forepaw. Svir felt himself staring. He daydreamed of encounters like this constantly, but now that he was confronted by reality he didn't know what to do or say. Tatja Grimm was certainly not pretty: she was beautiful, beautiful in an especially wonderful way. From a distance she would have appeared to be a slender girl with a superb figure and reddish brown hair. But Tatja Grimm was more than six feet tall—nearly as tall as Svir himself. Her hands were slim and delicate—and larger than the hands of most men. But the most wonderful thing of all was the look of genuine interest and intelligence in her gray-green eyes. She was interested in him.

"And your name?" Tatja smiled dazzlingly.

The wheels went round and Svir remembered his name: "Svir Hedrigs."

Tatja rubbed Svir's pet about the neck. "And that," spoke Svir, happy at finding something to say, "is Ancho."

"A dorfox? They're awfully rare, aren't they?"

"Uh-huh. Only a few can survive ocean voyages."

Tatja played with Ancho for a few seconds. The dorfox responded with satisfied humming. The human female was accepted.

Svir's hopes were shattered almost as quickly as they had crystallized. Three men came over and sat down, without a word to him.

"Miss Grimm, did you . . . ?" one began. Then he noticed the dorfox. The newcomers sat silently and watched her and the animal. Svir didn't know what was going on, but now he didn't care. There was obviously more competition here than he could handle.

Tatja Grimm looked up from the dorfox. "Men, this is Svir Hedrigs. Svir, meet Brailly Tounse, Rey Guille, and Kederichi Maccioso. They are respectively the First Proofreader, General Fiction Editor, and Ship's Captain for *Fantasie* magazine. I serve as the Science Editor."

Like hell, thought Svir. He knew he was being taken. He was a naturally gullible person. Once, in this very tavern, a couple of netscrapers had managed to convince him they were hot-air balloonists. Since then, he had been always on his guard. There were several good reasons why his new "friends" were frauds. In the first place, the Tarulle Publishing Barge wasn't due in the Krirsarque area for another three days. Svir had been very upset to learn that his ship would stay a day ahead of the Tarulle fleet as the publishing company sailed slowly east along the Chainpearl Archipelagate. He wouldn't receive the latest copies of *Fantasie*—all two years' worth—until he reached Bayfast in Crownesse. In the second place, the Tarulle Barge rarely landed at minor places like Krirsarque. The Barge dispatched its hydrofoil sailing boats for such contacts. These boats delivered the company's publications—and took aboard supplies and manuscripts. People like Rey Guille and Ked Maccioso were far too important and busy to leave the Barge. The frauds at his table had aimed far too high in their impersonation. Of all the literary corporations in the world—fiction or nonfiction, periodical or book—*Fantasie* was perhaps the most prestigious. Svir had always admired Rey Guille and the managing editor, Spektr Ramsey. And never had he seen a science section in *Fantasie,* or heard of Tatja Grimm.

Well, he determined, *I can trade them lie for lie* Aloud he said, "So happy to meet you. I find a lot of your stuff especially provocative since my specialty is astronomy."

"An astronomer?" They were obviously impressed. Even the over-muscled bruiser identified as Ked Maccioso seemed interested.

"That's right," Svir affirmed. And, actually, he was an astronomer. But the others naturally assumed from his unmodified assertion that he was one of those intrepid souls who manned the 60-inch reflector in the Doomsday Mountains on The Continent. Life at the Doomsday observatory was a constant struggle against asphyxiation, cold, mountain apes, and Hurdic tribesmen. "I came out here to deliver some speeches at Krirsarque University." This last was an inversion of the truth. Svir was a graduate student in astronomy at Krirsarque. For the last two years he had worked with the thirty-inch telescope at the university. The most recent publisher coming west from The Continent had brought news that the men at Doomsday had duplicated some of Svir's work, and now he had to journey all the way to the coast of The Continent to meet with one of the Doomsday astronomers and thrash the problem out.

"What's your preference in astronomy?" asked Tatja. "Seraphy?"

"No," replied Svir. "Seraph's not visible from Doomsday. I'm in a new field—parallax astronomy. Using very delicate trig techniques, I've measured the distances to some of the nearer stars."

"Really! I bought an article on that very subject for the latest issue." She snapped her fingers. "Brailly Tounse" reached into a side pouch and handed Tatja a magazine. She gave it to Svir. "See."

Svir gasped. There was the familiar masthead of *Fantasie*. In small letters beneath it were the words: "Issue of the 162nd Meridian. Whole Number 10,039." Here was physical proof that the Tarulle fleet had already arrived.

The cover was a Togoto pastel, at least the equal of that artist's Lindolef study. Svir opened it to the table of contents. Beneath the magazine's famous motto, "Things are not as they seem," were listed fifteen stories and novelettes by authors from all over the world, including new work by Ivam Alecque and Tsumish Kats. Svir flipped through the pages and came across one that caught on his fingers. It wasn't made of the usual seaweed pulp, but of some heavier, lacquer-coated material. At the top of that page was written: "Meet the *Fantasie* staff." Below were six portraits done in tones of green. But they weren't acid-etch prints, or even hand paintings. Those pictures were green-tinted windows revealing perfect likenesses of Tatja Grimm and the men seated at Svir's table.

He wondered if he looked as embarrassed as he felt. These people were everything they claimed to be. And now Tatja Grimm was even more desirable—if that were possible—than she had been before the others appeared.

Tatja placed her hand on his forearm as she saw what he was looking at. "How do you like those pictures? That's a development we picked up in the Osterlai Archipelagate. Those pictures are made by a machine that looks at its subject and instantly 'paints' the picture, just like in the Diogens stories." She slipped her hand down onto his. For a moment Svir's vision blurred. A warm glow spread through his body. "My picture is at the bottom there because the Science Department was only introduced last year, when dear old Spektr gave in to the increased popularity of contrivance fiction. . . . How long have you been acquainted with *Fantasie?*"

"Ever since I took some lit courses in triform school. Ten years. The Tarulle Barge has come through the Archipelagate five times in that period. I've looked forward to each arrival more and more eagerly. I've worked part time for the National Library's Restoration Department."

Tatja laughed, a friendly, intimate chuckle. The men at the table receded into the far back of Svir's consciousness. "That's a worthwhile job. Do you know that in all Tu, there is only one complete collection of *Fantasie?*"

"You mean the proof copies on the Barge?"

"No. Not even the Tarulle Company has a complete version. Remember, there was a fire on Old Barge three hundred years ago, and all the copies to that date were lost. Up to twenty years ago there were more than twenty-five complete collections, but a series of accidents has destroyed all but one." She put a faint accent on the word "accidents."

Svir had never thought about it, but it certainly was possible that only one complete collection existed. As the Tarulle Company toured the world, they sold their magazines and printed extra copies to drop off at later island chains. Delivery was quite unreliable compared to a subscription service—such as some island magazines used. Thus it was very difficult to get a continuous sequence of issues. And *Fantasie* was seven hundred years old. Even though most issues had been recopied and their stories anthologized, so that any major library contained thousands of stories from the magazine, there were still "lost" issues unavailable on the Chainpearls.

The person or government that possessed the complete set must be very wealthy and dedicated to culture. "Who has the collection?" asked Svir.

"The regent of Crownesse, Tar Benesh," Tatja answered.

Svir frowned. Tar Benesh had never impressed him as a man with deep cultural roots. He almost missed what Tatja Grimm said next. She wasn't looking directly at him, and her lips barely moved. She seemed to be preoccupied with something far away.

"It's too bad Benesh is going to destroy them."

"What! Why? Can't he be stopped?" His shocked questions tumbled over each other. Why would anyone want to destroy seven hundred years of *Fantasie?* The epic cycles, the ingenious short stories—all those glimpses into worlds-that-are-not—would be lost. Half the faculty of Arts and Letters at Krirsarque University would suicide.

Tatja's hand tightened around his. Her face came near to his and he heard her say, "Perhaps there is a way to stop him. With you and your dorfox perhaps—"

"Please, Miss Grimm, not here!" Ked Maccioso leaned forward tensely, at the same time glancing around the tavern. Svir's domain of attention expanded. He realized that now the Arbor was crowded, the dance floor overflowing, and the jongleurs in fine form on their resonation platform. Tatja's presence had made him completely unaware of the changes.

She nodded to the heavy Ship's Captain. "I suppose you're right, Ked." She turned back to Svir. "When were you planning to return to The Continent?"

Return? Then Svir remembered the lie he had told them. But he couldn't reveal his fraud to her now. He wanted, needed, the interest Tatja was showing him.

"I sail tomorrow for Bayfast."

"Would you like to come on the Tarulle Barge? It's slower than hydrofoil, but we'll get you there just the same."

"I certainly would." The words came spontaneously, but he felt no desire to retract them. Imagine sailing off with a beautiful, famous girl—into adventure. His previous reality seemed pale indeed beside these prospects.

"Why don't you come out to the Barge with us tonight. We'll show you around." She looked straight into his eyes. The men with her watched carefully, too. They couldn't talk here.

"Okay." Svir set Ancho on his shoulder. They all stood up and worked their way to the door. The music and party sounds faded as they descended the ancient stone stairs that led from Highrock to the wharves of the Krirsarque harbor.

Soon Maccioso was paddling them out to sea. Apparently the landing was a secret. It was well into the night sleep period and no other craft were moving. A breeze swept across the water, splashed luminescing algae into the boat.

Half an hour passed. No one spoke. Ancho shivered quietly, fearful of the water. They left the glowing waters of the harbor behind. It was quite cloudy, so even the light of Seraph was denied them. Gradually Svir convinced himself that there was a greater darkness on the water ahead of them. And then he was sure. The huge pile of the Tarulle Publishing Barge rose tier upon tier out of the ocean. Beside it floated the smaller forms of scout hydrofoils. All were without lights.

They pulled over to the hulk, and a group of company sailors pulled the little boat into a freight bay. A section leader saluted Maccioso. She said, "XO's compliments, sir, and no exterior activity noted."

Maccioso returned the salute. "Have him take us out past the shelf."

Svir was escorted up a long corridor, into the heart of the vessel. They entered a luxurious, brightly lit room. Just the maintenance of the algae pots must cost several man-hours a day. The five seated themselves around a table, on which was fastened a detailed map of Bayfast, the capital of Crownesse.

"This must all seem a bit melodramatic, Svir," spoke Tatja, "but Tar Benesh has an efficient spy system extending from Crownesse on The Continent all the way to the Osterlai Archipelagate. The Regent is ambitious without limit. He—"

Ancho began nibbling at the map. As Svir pulled him back, the animal keened an almost inaudible whistle. For an instant everyone in the room felt stark terror. Then Svir patted the little animal, and the dorfox relaxed. The feeling of panic disappeared. Ancho turned his large eyes toward Svir as if to ask forgiveness.

Tatja smiled shakily. "Tar Benesh is also an extremely intelligent, capable individual. And he is—mad. Or perhaps he is just alien. Some rumors hint that he is actually a Wildman from the center of The Continent.

"Since he came to power twenty years ago, he has been a collector of *Fantasie*. And to enhance the value of his wealth, we believe that he sabotaged other collections."

"We know for a *fact* that he has destroyed other collections," Rey Guille interrupted.

"Every five years Benesh holds the Festival of the Ostentatious Consumption. You may have heard of it. . . ."

Svir gulped. "You're not trying to tell me that the *Fantasie* collection is going to be one of the sacrifices?"

Tatja nodded her head slowly, "Yes, that's it exactly. The Festival is scheduled to begin ten days from now. We plan to arrive in Bayfast on the night wake period of the Consumption." She gestured to the map of the Bayfast area and the detailed floor plans of Tar Benesh's Keep. "I can't go over the details of the plans now, but we are going to try to save that collection. Our magazine has the unconditional backing of the entire Tarulle Company"—she nodded at Maccioso—"in this venture. It's not going to be easy But I think we could succeed if we had Ancho's help. And we need you too. You know Ancho best, and can persuade him to cooperate."

Svir glanced down at the little mammal, who sat licking his paws, unaware of the plans being made for him. "Yes," he answered, "dorfoxes are strange that way. They will answer to only one or two masters at a time. And no one can predict exactly when they will change loyalties."

"Svir, this will be dangerous. But we need you. And some of the stories Benesh has exist nowhere else. Will you come with us and help?" She was pleading.

Svir suddenly realized what he was being asked to do. He could get killed—and all for some magazines. Before now he had been uneasy at the mere thought of traveling to Crownesse, and now he was going to risk his life in a plot against the government of that country. Some sensible element within him was screaming *No—no—no*! But he saw the pleading in Tatja's eyes. He was hooked. "Yes," he quavered, then continued more strongly, feigning confidence, "I'll be glad to do anything I can."

"Wonderful!" spoke Tatja. She stood up. "Now I'm sure you'll want to go ashore and get your stuff together. Ked will have a boat take you back." The group left the room and walked toward the outer hull. About halfway there, Tounse and Guille left them for the typeset area. The walk gave Svir time for some heart-stopping second thoughts. He had a vivid imagination and it was working overtime now. Ancho responded uneasily to his fright, moving nervously on his neck.

They reached the landing bay, and Maccioso went off to get a crew. Tatja turned to Svir. She grasped his hand gently and moved close. "Thank you, Svir. *Fantasie* is the most valuable artwork in the world. I want to save that collection very much. But I think I want to see you again even more. You'll be back tomorrow, won't you?"

She slipped her arms around him. He felt her body against his, her lips against his. His fears and half-conscious plans to junk the whole project were erased. He would be back.

CHAPTER 2

It was well past midmorning. Svir stood—with Ancho on his shoulder—at the edge of the false deck that reinforced the Barge's bowform. Tatja had said she'd meet him here and take him on a tour.

The Tarulle Barge was especially impressive by day. Over the centuries, it had grown without any overall plan. New barge platforms had been added and built upon—then built over again until the mass resembled nothing so much as a man-made mountain of terraces, cupolas, and cranes. The top offices and printshops were of spun glass—the most modern construction material. The bottommost members of the Barge were mouldering timbers three hundred years old. From the top of the main mast to the bottom of the lowest hold was almost three hundred feet.

Now the huge filmy sails were close-hauled as the Barge tacked in the thirty-mile-per-hour Monsoonal Drag that blew steadily off The Continent.

Svir grabbed the terrace rail to steady himself in the wind. Just looking up at those masts was enough to make him dizzy. He turned his attention to the ocean and the whitecapped waves that stretched out to the horizon. In winds like this, the sailing hydrofoils were at top efficiency, getting up to almost fifty miles per hour. Two Company scouts cut through the farther waters as they sailed out to minor ports of the Chainpearl Archipelagate

And the Tarulle fleet was not alone on the main. Svir could pick out three cargo barges at various distances. The Chainpearls lay along one of the busiest trade routes on Tu.

For all their cultural importance, the publishing lines accounted for only a small fraction of total ocean tonnage.

Most publishing enterprises were operated landside, and contracted with freighting companies to serve other islands. Relatively rare were the huge publishing barges, like Tarulle, which toured the entire world and printed a variety of books and magazines.

"Hey, Svir!" Tatja's voice came clearly over the wind. He turned to see her striding toward him. Her hair was caught in a soft reddish swirl tied with a clip to the front of her tunic. Even so the wind blew it back and forth to caress the side of her face. She seemed small and delicate even in her baggy work coveralls, but when she came near, her eyes were level with his. Her smile sent a long shiver down his spine.

"I'm sorry we couldn't get together earlier in the morning," she continued, "but things are really moving around here. This Chainpearl run is always the busiest of the circuit, and when we have Monsoon winds, every printer is running at the breaking point."

"Uh, that's all right—I've had plenty to see," he replied. As a matter of fact, the wake period had been something of a bore so far. The crew was distinctly hostile toward nonessential personnel. Since lunch he had wandered about the decks. His ears still burned from insults received when he walked in a door marked TRIPULATION ONLY. These people weren't really stranger-haters, though. They just didn't want nonprofessionals messing up their work.

Svir and Tatja started toward a nearby stairway. She looked at the dorfox. "Say, I'm glad you brought Ancho. He looks fine. Can I carry him? We'll have to be real careful: some of the areas I'll show you could affect him. But I want to see how hardy he is."

Svir handed the dorfox over. Ordinarily the little animal didn't enjoy being fondled by others, but he had taken a shine to Tatja. Ancho had recovered from his initial fear of sailing, though even now he clutched at Tatja's shoulders more tightly than was necessary to maintain his perch. Dorfoxes came from a single island far around the world. They were long-lived and relatively infertile. Most dorfoxes became mortally seasick when taken aboard a ship. Ancho was an exception. Betrog Hedrigs, the great Continental explorer and Svir's grandfather, had brought the animal to Krirsarque forty years before. Ancho was probably the only dorfox in the Chainpearls. Perhaps it was just as well, though, for if dorfoxes were common, they would have turned society upside down. Their strange abilities would give criminals almost supernatural powers.

Svir and Tatja descended two flights to the vat holds. It was a different world: the inside of a claustrophobe's nightmare. The wind was no longer audible, but there was an ominous creaking from the hull of the barge platform. Dim orange light filtered from half-dead algae pots. Worst of all was the smell. Svir had been raised near the ocean, and so was virtually unaware of any special odor associated with the seas. But here, in these vats, the essence of those smells was being distilled.

Some of the workers actually smiled at them: Tatja's presence was safe conduct.

Tatja pointed to where the ocean water came in through the bowform. "The whole papermaking operation runs at just the speed that water can flow through these hulls. We're at the input now. If we walk to the stern, we'll see every stage of the processing."

The seawater flowed through the underpart of the Barge like a subterranean river. Narrow catwalks hung inches above the dark water. Every forty feet they had to climb up a short flight of steps and then down again, as they moved from the hull of one barge platform to the next. They walked about two hundred feet through the gloom. Svir admired the graceful way Tatja moved along the catwalk, and cursed his own fearful, halting pace. Below them the liquid had thickened and now flowed slowly past grinding wheels. Beyond this it was divided into several streams, depending on which reagents were to be added to the conglomeration of sargasso, algae, and animalcules that composed the slimy mass. They followed the stream of sludge that was destined to become paper.

All the way, Tatja gave a running account of what was going on. She also kept a close eye on Ancho for any signs of nausea or disorientation. But the dorfox seemed quite calm. It was a different story for Svir. The stench was beginning to get to him. Finally he asked, "How can the hull take these chemicals? I should think it would rot in a matter of months."

"That's a good question," Tatja responded. "The processing seems to have just the opposite effect. The carbonates and silicates in this sludge replace the wood fiber on a microscopic level. Over the years the hull has actually become stronger. And what we discharge beneath the hull is so concentrated it kills any parasites that might otherwise nest there. Oops!"

She slipped on the walk. Svir's arm reached out and grabbed her waist as Ancho caught at his collar. The three of them teetered precariously for a moment. Then Tatja laughed nervously. "Thanks."

Svir felt obscurely proud. He might move more slowly than she, but when it came to a test, his caution paid off. He didn't remove his arm from her waist.

At last they reached the stern. Here the remaining water was pressed from the bleached sea mass, and the paper was actually formed. The fine sheets hung for several days before they were wound about drums and taken up to printing.

They walked up to the next deck, where tons of newly printed magazines were stored. Here too the light was dim, but there was only a faint musty smell. Thank God the final product didn't smell like seaweed, thought Svir.

Tatja hung close on his arm and became more talkative. The Tarulle company put out five different magazines every sixteen days. *Fantasie* and a couple of girlie magazines accounted for four hundred thousand copies per issue and provided the bulk of the Tarulle income. Since it was necessary to stock copies for as long as two years before they were sold, the Barge normally carried eight hundred tons of magazines. Over the centuries it had been a race to keep up with world population increase. The Barge was now more than ten times as large as its first platform. All the latest machinery was employed. But even with increased landside printing and the prospect of writing machines to replace hand typesetting, they were still falling behind.

They came to one of the loading ports. The sound of the wind came strong, and beyond that huge hole in the hull was a panorama of sky and sea. Less than twenty feet away floated one of the fifty-ton hydrofoils that did most of the delivery work for the Barge. Its sails were reefed and its boom masts were in the vertical position, permitting it to move closer to the larger vessel. A fifteen-ton load of magazines was being hoisted onto the hydrofoil by one of the Barge's cranes.

They watched the scene for several minutes. Finally the operation was complete, and the boat pushed away from the Barge. Its booms were lowered and the sails—like sheets on a clothesline—were hung out. As it moved out of the Barge's wind shadow, it gathered speed, and the outermost studding sails tilted queerly into the wind. The whole affair lifted up on the slender stilts of its foils, and the boat moved away at nearly forty miles an hour. Then the Barge's crewmen closed the loading port and everything was dim again.

Tatja frowned. "You know, I've always wondered why they tilt the studding sails like that."

Svir grinned broadly and gave her an explanation of Dertham's pressure theories, complete with an analogy to tacking. Her eyes showed scarcely concealed admiration. "You know, Svir, that's the first clear explanation I've ever heard of that. You ought to try writing it up. I could use some decent articles."

"Try me," said Svir. Then he noticed the dorfox. "He's glazing over," he said, indicating the animal's eyes.

Tatja agreed, "So I see. We better cut things short. It's almost supper time anyway. We'll just take a short look at the print deck, and leave the typeset and editorial offices for another time."

They went up another stairway and entered a low room filled with whirling gears. Svir wondered if all vessels were this crowded. It destroyed the romantic air he had always associated with sailing. He noticed that Tatja kept a close hold on the dorfox and petted him comfortingly. This was no place for Ancho to run about unprotected.

There were two machines in the room, but only one of them was in operation. At one end of the printer, a yard-wide roll of sea-paper unwound and slid between two rotating drums. The upper drum was inked, and with every swift revolution it pressed at least twelve feet of print on the flowing paper. Beyond this first pair of drums, a second pair did the same for the underside of the sheet. The paper finally moved under a whirling glass flywheel that cut it into neat, yard-square sheets that landed in a small dolly, ready to be taken to the cutting and binding section. The machine was driven by a spinning shaft connected to the windmills on the main deck.

One of the printmen looked up angrily and started toward them. Then he recognized Tatja, and his manner changed. Up close, Svir saw that the ink-stained face belonged to Brailly Tounse. "Day, ma'am," Tounse shouted over the din. "Anything we can do for you?"

"Well, if you have a couple of minutes, could you describe your operation, Brailly?"

Tounse seemed momentarily surprised, but agreed. He took them down the print line and traced the progress of the paper through the machine. "Right now we're doing almost five thousand impressions an hour—that's about one hundred thousand pages after cutting. Sometimes we go for months with hardly a breeze, but when we move into the Drag we have to make up for every minute of it. I'm pushing these machines at their physical limit right now. If you could get us just two hundred ounces of steel, Miss Grimm, we could make some decent bearings, and run these things as fast as the wind can blow—about twelve thousand impressions an hour." He looked at Tatja expectantly.

She smiled and shouted back, "Brailly, I'll bet there isn't a thousand ounces of steel in the whole Barge."

Svir was confused. Since when does a chief proofreader ask a science editor for mechanical help—and for something as ridiculous as steel! Perhaps the fellow was just teasing, though he certainly looked serious enough.

Tounse grimaced, wiped his greasy hand over his bald head, leaving a broad black streak. The man was obviously exhausted. "Well," he said, "you might as well stick around and see them install a new print board on the other machine." He indicated the idle printer.

Several crewmen brought in four yard-square sheets of rubbery printboard. The elastic base made it possible for them to stretch the type across the drum and fasten down the edges. The ironwood-sap type pieces gleamed dully in the light. In a few moments they would be black with ink. When the first four sheets were properly tied down, the workers moved down the line and tacked four more on the underside printer. Then they hand fed twenty feet of roll paper through the machine.

Tounse nodded to the man at the clutch. The gearing engaged. Perhaps the fellow released the clutch too fast. Or perhaps the gearing was fatigued. Svir never knew the exact cause, but the machine was transformed into a juggernaut. Gears splintered and paper billowed wildly about him. The first print drum precessed madly and then flew off its spindle, knocking all three of them against the first machine. The glass blade at the far end of the room shattered, and slivers flew about the room. Even though declutched, the machinery took seconds to slow and stop.

Svir picked himself up carefully. Tounse was all right, though he seemed on the verge of breaking down himself—printing machines just weren't supposed to behave like this! Svir dragged Tatja from beneath the drums. She sat up and looked at him, dazed.

"Svir, are you all—where's Ancho!"

The dorfox was gone. Tatja swore in a most unladylike manner. She picked herself up and declutched the first machine. "Tounse! Forget your damn machines. We've got to find that animal." Soon Tounse and his whole work gang were searching the printrooms for Ancho. Svir wondered briefly if the dorfox could be deceiving them all with an I'm-not-here signal. Ancho hadn't pulled a trick like that in five years. And there was no special motive for him to do so now. If Ancho had not been killed in the mangle, he was probably scared witless. His panic, combined with his general fear of the sea, had probably driven him outside and to some higher deck.

Svir left the others and ran outside. He glanced quickly about and ran up to the next level. Soon he had reached the mast deck. He stopped, gasping for breath. The wind was much stronger here. From the sails and rigging above him came a continuous, singing hum. He was alone except for a single sailor in a short semiskirt. She was climbing a rope ladder that stretched down from the main mast. Svir wondered what she was doing. The rigging was adjustable from down in the navigation section; besides, it was too windy to climb safely. Then he looked up past the girl. Almost forty feet above her he saw Ancho's furry form. Svir ran across the deck, toward the main mast. The dorfox moved awkwardly up the rope. He had panicked completely. Dorfoxes are, at best, only fair climbers He was trying to retreat from all the things that frightened him, and up was the only direction left. Svir debated whether he should follow the sailor, then saw that it would just upset her precarious balance. The wind blew the ladder into a clean catenary form. As the sailor rose higher, she was forced to climb with her back to the ground and the rope above her. Ancho was radiating helpless distress—even down on the deck it made Svir faint with fear. Its effect on the sailor must have been nearly intolerable. For a heartstopping instant it looked as if she were going to fall. Her feet slipped from the rope and she hung by her hands from beneath the ladder. Then she hooked her leg around the ladder and inched forward. She was no longer climbing. One hundred fifty feet above the deck, the ladder was blown nearly horizontal.

Finally she reached Ancho. She seemed to coax him. The dorfox clutched at her neck, or the top of her shirt. The two came slowly down the long, curving ladder.

The girl collapsed at the base of the mast. Ancho released his tight hold on her and scuttled over to Svir.

Svir held the whimpering animal and helped the sailor to her feet. She was a bit taller than average, with black hair cut in short bangs. At the moment her face was very pale. "That was a brave thing you did," said Svir. Without doubt, she had saved the animal's life. "You really know how to handle those ropes."

The girl laughed weakly. "Not me. I'm an apprentice proofreader for the Llereno edition." She spoke in brief, anguished spurts. Her mind knew she was safe now, but her body did not. "That's the first time I ever climbed them. Oh God! Every time I looked down, I wanted to throw up. Everything looked so far away and hard."

She sat back down on the deck. She was shaking as much as Ancho. Svir put his hand on her shoulder.

"I like to come up here on my lunch time," she said. "Your pet came running across the deck like his tail was on fire. He just grabbed the ladder and climbed. I could tell he didn't like climbing, but he was terrified of whatever was chasing him. Every few rungs, he'd stop and try to come down. I—I just had to do something."

As she spoke these words, Tatja arrived on the mast deck. She ran over, and inspected Ancho with a careful, expert eye.

She didn't say anything for several seconds, though she favored the girl with a long, calculating glance. *Could Tatja be jealous?* thought Svir, surprised. The girl scrambled to her feet and bowed slightly to the science editor. Finally Tatja turned to Svir and smiled. "Svir Hedrigs, be introduced to Apprentice Proofreader Coronadas Ascuasenya. Coronadas Ascuasenya, Parallax Astronomer Svir Hedrigs."

"Pleased." The girl bowed again and smiled hesitantly.

"Tatja, Coronadas climbed almost to the top of the mast to save Ancho."

"Yes, we saw from down below. That was a brave rescue." She petted Ancho. "I just hope we haven't wrecked the dorfox. We were fools to take him along this morning." She looked up at the sun, which was just past the zenith. "We might as well get some dinner. It's too late to start any training. We can begin this evening." She picked up Ancho and they all descended to the lower decks.

CHAPTER 3

The sun was three hours down before they began. The night was clear and Seraph's light brought a bluish sheen to the sea. Tatja had used paperboard partitions to simulate a hallway within Benesh's Keep. She had constructed the mock-up on a portion of the deck out of the wind and hidden from the view of other ships.

"I'll admit it's pretty crude, Svir, but for the first trials we don't need anything elaborate. The dimensions are the same as inside the castle. You can see there are a couple of side passages opening off the main one."

Svir moved to the entrance of the maze. It certainly wasn't very convincing. The ceiling of the passage was purple sky. Posted at regular intervals down the forty-foot passage were company sailors simulating Royal Guardsmen. They didn't seem too certain of just what was expected of them.

Tatja petted Ancho gently. "We want Ancho to make these 'Guardsmen' hallucinate. It's going to take some training, but I want Ancho to convince whoever he points those pretty ears at that you and he constitute an authority figure."

Svir was surprised. "Is that possible? Ancho isn't very smart, you know. It seems to me that in order to generate a detailed illusion, Ancho would have to be humanly bright."

Tatja shook her pretty head. "Nope. The intelligence of the victim provides all the background detail. I've spent several months on Dorfox Island, and I know things like that are possible. C'mon, let's start, or we'll still be at it when we pull into Bayfast."

Ancho was sometimes sleepy during night wake periods, but he perked up noticeably when Tatja had a large bowl of rehydrated *klig* leaves brought on deck. He strained against Svir's hands, but he wouldn't let him at the leaves. The dorfox was going to have to earn his treats. Svir's father had often played games like this with Ancho, and had managed to teach him a number of tricks.

Svir stood up and put the dorfox on his shoulder. The "Guardsmen" had assumed their posts in the passageway. The only woman among them was Cor Ascuasenya, who stood at the far end of the mock-up. Tatja stood behind Svir. In this position she could watch what happened with relative impunity, since Ancho was not likely to turn around and broadcast in her direction.

"All right, Svir, give it a walkthrough. We'll see if Ancho will give us a demonstration," said Tatja.

Svir walked slowly through the mock-up. Everything seemed quite normal. But then, Ancho rarely aimed his hallucinations at his master. . . .

When he was through, Tatja asked the first sailor what he had seen.

The fellow looked at her a little blankly. "What do you mean? When are you going to start the test?" The others wre similarly confused. None of them had been conscious of Svir or Ancho as they walked down the hall. Tatja unfastened the lid on the *klig* bowl.

"That was a good performance," she said. "Ancho managed to scan every person as you walked past. Now we have to make him try his other effects, till he produces exactly what we're looking for." She fed Ancho two leaves. The little mammal sucked on them greedily, momentarily enraptured. When he was done he reached out for more, but Tatja had already relocked the basket. He had done well, but a larger award must await an even better performance.

Svir petted Ancho, who appeared to enjoy the game. "You know, Tatja, Ancho is really dependable with that I'm-not-here signal. And he can scan a lot of people at once. Why don't you settle for that, without trying for something more sophisticated?"

"It's not enough, Svir. You're going to have to go all the way to the center of the Keep—to the vault where the most precious sacrifices are kept. With Ancho's I'm-not-here, you *probably* could steal the Guards' keys. But what if some of the doors have combination locks? You need more than the Guards' passive acceptance. They must actively help you. And there are more than ten thousand volumes in the *Fantasie* collection. That comes to at least two tons. You're going to need help getting them out." She picked up her noteboard and pen. "Let's try it again."

And again. And again.

Ancho soon learned that anything he tried would earn him some reward, but that if he repeated a previous performance, the prize was smaller. So he tried to come up with a new effect on each try. They soon exhausted the natural dorfox responses—the instinctive responses which served so well on the dorfox's native island. Some of these could drive predators away or dull their senses. Others attracted insects and lulled their suspicions.

Ancho also tried the tricks he had been taught since arriving in civilization. On one pass all the crewmen in the passage broke into fits of hysterical laughter. Cor Ascuasenya had the giggles fifteen minutes after Ancho came by. What they saw was hilariously funny, though they couldn't explain to Tatja and Svir just why.

Though Tatja did her best to pace the work, the project became a grind. The sailors were especially tired. Ancho had put them through an emotional wringer. In one twenty-minute period he made then laugh and cry. He had responded eagerly to all the attention showered upon him, but now was beginning to lose interest.

For the hundredth time Svir started down the mock passageway. He was surprised at the degree of respect and obedience these sailors showed Tatja. She must have more authority on the Barge than her title indicated. When she made a suggestion in her low, pleasant voice, people jumped. It was evidence of how the best people rose to the top in any organization. What had he done to deserve her?

But it was beginning to look as though she was wrong about Ancho. Apparently this was one trick the dorfox couldn't do. Maybe it was just as well. Svir wasn't really eager to stick his nose into the business of Tar Benesh.

"Damn it, man, stand up straight when you walk!" It took Svir an astonished second to realize that Tatja was speaking to him. "Come back and start over. How can you expect the dorfox to cast an illusion of authority if you drag about like an addled tri-form student?"

Svir bit back a sharp reply. He walked to the beginning and started over. He almost swaggered down the passageway, imitating the gait of a Crownesse bureaucrat he had once seen at a university dinner in Krirsarque. The effect was subtle. Suddenly he was no longer pretending. He actually felt important and powerful—the way he had always imagined politicians and generals must feel. It seemed only natural that the sailors should snap to attention as he passed them. He returned their brace with an informal salute. The feeling of power disappeared when he came to the end of the passage.

Tatja smiled. "Wow! All right, Miss Ascuasenya, just what did you see when Svir walked by you?"

Cor looked confused. She glanced from Tatja to Svir and back again. "When I first looked at him coming down the hall, I could have sworn it was my father—but my family is in the Llerenito Archipelagate! Closer, I saw that it was Jespen Tarulle. I mean, I knew it was Svir—it had to be. But it was Jespen Tarulle at the same time. Even now when I look at him, I see Tarulle—and yet I see Svir, too." Svir glanced as Ancho's ears. They weren't pointing at Cor. The hallucination persisted even after the dorfox stopped radiating.

Tatja didn't say anything for a second. She made a couple of notes in her book and looked up. "Can you see Ancho sitting on Svir's shoulder?"

Cor squinted. "No. All I see is that queer double image I just described."

The others had similar reactions. About half saw Svir as Tatja. These people were especially confused, since they now saw *two* Tatja Grimms. Every one of them realized that Ancho's trickery was involved, and all but two could see Svir behind the hallucination.

Svir's shoulders sagged. All that work, and the best they could come up with was a half-baked illusion that wasn't even uniform. It would never fool the Royal Guards.

But Tatja seemed to feel otherwise. She finished writing in the notebook and looked up, smiling. "Well, we've done it. The illusion is one of the strongest I've ever seen. It persists even in the face of contradiction-to-fact situations.

See, Svir, all you have to do is *act* confident. Ancho knows you and will radiate the same thing. I really didn't mean to jump on you."

Svir nodded, still blushing from the unexpected attack. Her technique worked, but it was shocking.

Tatja continued, "We'd better knock off now. Ancho's beginning to lose interest. By now he's crammed full of *klig* leaves. And most of you look pretty dragged out. Let's have another session after lunch."

During the rest of the voyage to Bayfast they had four hours of practice in every wake period. In the end Ancho was able to broadcast the authority signal even better than he could the I'm-not-here. He also grew fat on the *klig* leaves, assuming an almost spherical form. Tatja had him perform his new trick under every conceivable condition—even in the dark, down in one of the holds. They found that if a single authority figure were suggested to all the victims, then they all saw that same person. It took Ancho only a fraction of a second to set up the illusion in the human mind, and it persisted without booster treatment for almost ten minutes. Ancho could detect people hiding behind bulkheads, and could even project the authority illusion through several feet of stone. Tatja tried several times to make the dorfox generate the illusion for her, but he just purred when she held him. One experiment was a mystery to Svir. Tatja produced a flat *balsir* box and strapped it to Ancho's back. He didn't seem to mind; the box was light and apparently the straps didn't chafe. The contraption looked vaguely like an oversize cookie cutter—its profile was an irregular set of semicircles and lines. From either side of the box projected stubby cylinders of glass and wood. On top was a little hole—like the keyhole in a spring-powered clock. And the device clicked almost like a clock when it was mounted on Ancho's back.

Tatja refused to reveal the exact purpose of the contraption. She said it was a last precaution, one whose usefulness would be impaired if Svir knew its purpose. He couldn't imagine what sort of precaution would have such properties, but he accepted her explanation. Perhaps it was empty—a placebo to give him the false confidence necessary to trigger Ancho's authority signal. But whatever it was, it was for the best—Tatja wanted it.

The Drag kept Tatja busy—even busier than the general run of the crew. Besides their practice sessions, Svir was with her only two or three hours out of every wake period. He saw almost as much of the proofreader, Coronadas Ascuasenya. It was surprising how often he found her eating at the same time and in the same meal hall as he. He came to enjoy those meals more and more. Cor was no competition for Tatja, but she was pretty and intelligent and nice to be with.

Svir spent the rest of his free time in the Barge library, where Tatja's influence had opened some otherwise locked doors. Only fifteen or twenty people out of the thousand on board were allowed access to the library, but once inside there was no restriction on the use of materials. Here Tarulle kept specimen copies of all available issues of magazines published by the company. That amounted to about one hundred thousand volumes. Jespen Tarulle was in the printing business to make money, but he had a sense of history too, and the Barge library was the most luxurious part of the craft that Svir had yet seen. Here was none of the cramped stuffiness of the lower decks. Virtually none of the sea or ship noises were audible through the thick glass window. Deep carpets covered the floor. During the night wake periods, well-tended algae pots supplemented Seraph's light.

To a confirmed *Fantasie* addict, it was heaven. The Tarulle collection was nearly three quarters complete —more than seven thousand issues. That was better than any library on the Chainpearls. There were several copies of the first issue, printed just forty years after the invention of movable type. In those years the magazine was sold in two yard-square sheets, folded into quarters. Only rarely was a story illustrated, and then it was with crude woodcuts. But that was part of the enchantment. On a single barge—the predecessor of the present compound Barge—they had printed such works as *Delennor's Doom* and *Search for the Last Kingdom,* novels that after seven hundred years were still studied by poets and read with enjoyment by near illiterates. The genius which showed through those smudged pages transcended the vehicle that had brought it across time to the present.

That original barge had been owned by an ambitious trading family distantly related to the present publisher, Tarulle. At first they confined their trade to the major islands of the Osterlai group—and at the same time provided regular and vital communication between those islands. As the business became more profitable, the family gave up their other trading operations and visited islands further and further asea. The islands beyond the horizon provided even more enchanting themes and original authors. *Fantasie* readers were the first (and for a long time the only) cosmopolitans on the planet.

The magazine's success was not without social repercussions. The effects of the first interplanetary fantasy were shattering both for the magazine and for the rules of the Llerenito Archipelagate. *Migration* by Ti Liso forecast the rise of contrivance fiction. Liso's hero discovered a species of flying fish, which during the winter season in the northern hemisphere migrated to the southern hemisphere of Seraph. The hero captured several of the vicious creatures and taught them to pull his sailing boat. After a two-week flight the fish deposited him half-starved on the south polar continent of Seraph. The story went on to describe the civilization he found there. It was an unfortunate coincidence that Liso's Seraphian government was an absurd dictatorship founded on Tu-worship—for the tyrannical government of the Llerenitos was just such a farce in reverse. In plain fact the story had not been intended as satire. It had been written as straight adventure. Liso, a native of the Osterlais, had honestly conceived the most ridiculous autarchy imaginable. The Seraphiles of the Llerenitos did not take it as a joke, and for the next fifty years, until the fall of their religion, Llerenito waters were forbidden to the barge. This was an especial hardship, since the technique for sailing to the windward was not fully developed at that time. Avoiding the Llerenitos cost many months sailing time.

Each day brought Svir closer to the coast of The Continent, closer to Bayfast. Back in Krirsarque, the prospect of invading the Crownesse Keep had seemed a faraway adventure. But now he was coming to realize that it was a reality which he personally would have to face. More and more he spent his time in the library—in retreat from the nightmare that approached. He had always found refuge in *Fantasie,* and now he dived into the more recent stories with a vengeance. Sometimes he could avoid thinking of his own problems for hours at a time. He enjoyed the recent stories most. Especially contrivance fiction. The straight fantasy themes had been handled in every conceivable way in the past seven hundred years. It was only in the last two hundred that the idea of physical progress had emerged—the idea that there could be mechanical means of achieving fantastic ends. In the last fifteen years nearly half of *Fantasie*'s output had been cf.

Hedrigs read straight through Tsumish Kats's new serial. Kats was a biologist in the Tsanart Archipelagate. His science was usually strong and this novel was no exception. Like many authors, he postulated the discovery of large metallic deposits on The Continent. Such deposits made possible the construction of huge metal machines—machines powered by the same as-yet-unexplained mechanism that made the sun shine. As far as Svir could tell, this story contained a genuinely original idea—one that he wished he had thought of first. Instead of going directly to Seraph in his metal "ships of space," Kats set up way stations, tiny artificial moons.

The ultimate landing on Seraph produced deadly peril. Kats populated the other planet with a race of intelligent germs. Svir choked—this fellow was supposed to be a biologist? But on the next few pages the author actually justified the alien existence in a manner quite as logical and novel as his space-island idea. Svir found himself following the story more and more avidly as the human race fought to protect itself from the menace brought back aboard the landing ship. The struggle against the microscopic invaders was one of the most suspenseful he had ever read. Things looked hopeless for humankind. . . . He turned the page.

The dirty bastard! Svir's comfortable shell of illusion burst. Kats had actually let the human race fall before the invaders! He suppressed a desire to rip the magazine up into small pieces. The shock was like finding a snake in a *schnafel* pastry. Wasn't there enough hell in the real world? He had seen far too many stories of this type lately. Feeling quite betrayed to reality by Messrs Ramsey and Kats, the young astronomer stood up and stomped out of the library.

He stopped on the terrace-deck near his cabin. It was past midday. Far above him the wind whistled through the empty rigging and mastwork. Just two miles away the brown and gray cliffs of Somnai rose abruptly from the ocean, hiding Bayfast from view. Where the surf smashed into the base of Somnai, the concentrated coastal plankton formed a glistening green band. In this longitude Seraph hung almost thirty degrees above the horizon, its bluish-green crescent wraithlike against the bright blue sky.

The scene didn't appeal. Svir cupped his chin in his palm and morosely inspected the pitted guard railing he leaned against. For all practical purposes they had reached Bayfast. Right now Kederichi Maccioso was treating with the Port Commander for landing clearance. Apparently there was some problem about getting pier space at this time, but this would be cleared up, and come this afternoon they would be sailing right past the Regent's Keep into the Hidden Harbor. And tonight he, Svir Hedrigs, would be risking his life to save the *Fantasie* collection. Could he go through with it?

CHAPTER 4

He didn't notice her until she was at the railing beside him.

"Hi, Cor."

"Hi." She smiled. They stood for a moment silently, watching the sparkling sea. Then she said hesitantly, "It's tonight, isn't it?"

"Yeah." Casually.

"Svir . . . don't go through with it."

"Huh?" He looked at her in some confusion. "Why not?"

"Those magazines aren't worth dying for. And I think you *would* die. Crownesse is the most powerful country in the world. When we move into port, we'll pass Hangman's Row. They play rough here."

She was voicing the fears that had transformed these last few days into hell. Now if only she could convince him that it was honorable to back out. "I agreed to do it, Cor. And I owe it to Tatja."

Cor mumbled something.

"What's that?"

She took a deep breath and started over. "That second is not at all a reason. Tatja Grimm is . . . not a very nice person. She came aboard Tarulle only five years ago, as the Barge was passing through the Eastern Crownesse ports. She was an apprentice proofreader for Spräk editions. Now she is probably the most powerful person in the entire Tarulle Company—Jespen Tarulle included. She has some sort of leverage with every important person on the Barge. Some love her, I think. With others it's blackmail. Many people are just afraid of her. And no one knows what she's really after."

Svir scowled. "You can't expect me to believe that. I've

watched the crew working with her. She gets more wholehearted cooperation and respect from them than most officers." He felt the same hostility toward Cor that he would toward an outsider who slandered a member of his personal family.

Cor just looked tired. "That just proves she's a brilliant leader. I don't deny that. And she's at least as talented when it comes to mechanical matters, smarter than anyone I've ever seen. She designed the power trains they use in printing. She also developed some of the special sailing rigs we have on our hydrofoils."

Svir grunted, remembering a certain conversation several days earlier. But this thought was not reflected in the manner of his next question. "Just what brings you to spread this outrageous libel?"

She paled slightly. "I . . . I don't want you hurt, Svir. Tatja may not be precisely evil. But she is beyond my understanding. And I know that if it would further her ends, she'd put your life in jeopardy. Besides, I . . . want you myself." Her voice dropped almost to a whisper.

Svir felt himself soften. The things Cor had said became more understandable and more excusable. "I'm sorry, Cor. I didn't know you felt that way. But you're wrong. Tatja is wonderful. And I love her."

"No!" The response was violent. "Just let me show you. Can Ancho still broadcast that I'm-not-here signal?"

"Yeah." Svir petted the animal sitting on his shoulder. Ancho had seemed almost to enjoy the voyage during the last couple of days. "If he knows that something is expected of him and yet I don't pull that confidence act, he'll generally broadcast the I'm-not-here."

"Fine. Let's use him to do a little eavesdropping. I'll give you odds of five-to-one Tatja Grimm will be doing something you'd find out of character."

Svir was shocked by the vehemence of her assertion. Spying on others was an activity he had never condoned. He temporized. "It's kind of late, you know. She's probably asleep."

"Sleep? Sometimes I wonder if she does that." She caught his arm. "C'mon."

With an ugly sense of betrayal, he followed. Cor led him fifty yards aft and down a couple of flights. They were well into the day sleep period, and hardly anyone was about. The mast watch could detect any hostiles approaching the vessel, but they were not well placed for observing the deck itself.

Finally Svir and Cor stood below the balcony of Tatja's office. Svir cuddled Ancho. "Stay close to me up there, Cor, and you'll be inside the illusion, too." He boosted her up to the balcony, then hauled himself up. They had overextended themselves: it was just conceivable that people outside the illusion might be aware of them. But he was committed now.

They crawled to the office window and peeked over the sill. Svir was unprepared for the luxury of that room. It was almost as large as the library. The floor was carpeted with Lockspur jaguar pelts and the furniture inlaid with designs of worked silver—or that rarest of metals, aluminum.

Tatja sat at her desk, her face in profile. She was slumped over, studying a large sheet of paper on her desk. Svir had never seen her look quite so morose. Except for her size she might have been a child, outcast. Her eyes were wide and staring, and a tear glistened on her cheek. He leaned closer against the window. What was she reading that could be so depressing? The paper on her desk was a detailed engineering diagram of—what? Then he recognized it as one of the Osterlai plans for a steam-driven turbine. The engine was ingenious and quite workable—but many thousands of ounces of iron were necessary for its construction. Attempts to make boilers of nonmetallic materials had been comical, and occasionally disastrous, failures. How would an engineering diagram cause someone to cry?

Tatja looked up suddenly, not at the window, but at the door to her office. Apparently someone was asking admittance, though it was virtually impossible to hear anything through the thick glass. She moved with amazing speed to cover the diagram and compose her features. In a matter of seconds she appeared completely self-possessed. The visitor was Brailly Tounse. Svir pressed his ear against the glass, forgetting any scruples he had had about eavesdropping. What was said within was barely audible.

Tounse was saying, "Your people took fifteen ounces . . . steel. My steel! Why?"

"I needed it." Her expression was almost haughty.

But Tounse was not put off. "So? I . . . too. We can't run the presses without *some* metals, you . . ."

"Tough. We're . . . lee of the Somnai now, so it doesn't matter . . . return it after we leave Bayfast . . . need it to rescue . . . *Fantasie* collection."

This last promise seemed to mollify Tounse somewhat, but he still asked, ". . . really think . . . will go through with it?"

Tatja laughed. "I can persuade that fatuous idiot to . . . anything—you should know that." Tounse's face went red.

Svir drew back from the window, shocked. Were they talking about *him*? He looked at Cor and she returned his gaze levelly—she obviously thought so.

"Let's go," Svir muttered. He moved to the edge of the balcony and jumped to the deck below—almost on top of a crewman wearing editorial insignia. The fellow stared at him for a long moment and then continued his walk; apparently Ancho had stopped broadcasting. What if Tatja heard about this? The idea was chilling.

This line of thought was cut short as Cor came over the railing. They walked back toward the crew quarters. He stopped a few feet from the entrance to his own cabin.

Cor looked at him. "Well?"

"I don't know, Cor. Perhaps if I knew more, what we saw wouldn't be incriminating. I'm all confused."

"When do you have to make up your mind?"

"Sometime this evening. I'm going to have a final briefing before lunch in the night wake period. I don't know how long after that I'd be leaving."

"Don't go—at least think about what I said and what we saw." She looked at him. "Please."

Svir laughed harshly, "Girl, that's one thing you can be absolutely sure of!"

She touched his hand briefly, then turned and walked away.

Svir didn't get much sleep that afternoon. He lay on his

bunk in the shuttered cabin and stared into the darkness. What was Tatja Grimm? To him she had been a miraculous discovery, an escape from loneliness. And until now he had never doubted her sincerity. To the crew she was an immensely popular leader, one who could solve any problem. To the top officers on the Barge she was a harsh and arbitrary tyrant, a seductive genius, a bitch-goddess. Where did that leave the Tatja Grimm who sat silently, crying over an engineer's diagram?

In any case, Tatja was not what he had imagined. And that revelation put the present situation in a new light.

Though it was past sunset, he didn't go down for breakfast, but paced tensely back and forth in the little cabin. On the bed Ancho chirped and croaked miserably.

Svir had agreed to do a job. Only now did he realize just how much he had been influenced by Tatja. He saw that the rescue of the *Fantasie* collection was an extremely important project—but without the spell Tatja's personality had cast upon him, he felt no interest in committing his own skin to the undertaking. Art was art, but life was sacred—especially his life. If he went through with the plan, Svir Hedrigs would probably die tonight. And that death would not be the adventurous, romantic death of a hero, but a sick, empty, final thing. Just thinking about it gave him the chills. How close he had come to sacrificing himself for—nothing. If it hadn't been for Cor he would have, too. She was as true as Tatja was false. He had found out just in time.

He would turn Tatja down—the most she could get him for was his passage. She would have to find another sucker and another dorfox. He would see the Doomsday astronomer and get that situation cleared up. And perhaps—no, *certainly*—he would see Cor again, and ask her to leave Tarulle and come back to the Chainpearls with him.

Svir fed the dorfox a luscious meal, then went down to the main chow hall. He didn't see Cor. That was unusual, but not surprising. They were still working extra shifts, processing material. He would see her later in the evening, after he confronted Tatja. He whistled as he bounded up the steps, thinking of the look on Tatja's face when he told her he wasn't going to help her.

The Barge was entering Bayfast Harbor now. That entrance was a narrow gorge cutting through the Somnai cliffs. Seraph was nearly full, and its brilliant blue light transformed the normally brown cliffs into shimmery curtains of stone. Svir had to crane his neck to see the top, where the Bayfast naval guns were mounted, pointing down at him. The Tarulle Barge was almost half as wide as the entrance.

His stride broke as he noticed a small lighter pulling away from the Barge. That girl with the helmet of short black hair—she looked like Coronadas Ascuasenya. He rushed to the terrace rail. She was more than fifty yards away and not facing him—but he was almost sure it was Cor. On her lap she carried a small suitcase. What was going on? He ran along the rail, shouting her name. But the wind, channeled by the gorge, was loud, and she was already far away. The boat rounded the curve of the gorge, disappeared.

Perhaps it wasn't Cor after all, but the old *Fantasie* motto came to mind: "Things are not as they seem."

His mood was considerably subdued by the time he reached the executive decks. He confronted one of Tatja's secretaries and was ushered into the Science Editor's office.

Tatja smiled faintly as Svir advanced to her desk. "Have a seat, Svir. Ready to begin the briefing?"

Svir didn't accept the proffered chair. He stood awkwardly before the desk. Tatja's physical presence almost made him disregard what he had seen that afternoon, and suddenly it was difficult to say the speech he had been planning. "Tatja—Miss Grimm, I've been thinking, uh, about this . . . project. I know it's important to you—to everyone here. But I, uh, I don't think that I'm the right, uh . . ."

Tatja picked a crystal letter opener from her desk. She flashed him a broad smile. "To make a long story short, you've decided you would rather not go through with it. You're willing to pay for your passage, but you feel no obligation to risk your neck on this scheme. Is that what you are trying to say?"

"Why, yes," Svir said, relieved. "I'm glad you see my point of view."

Tatja didn't say anything. She inspected the letter opener, tossed it into the air in a glittering whirl, and caught it just before it would have slammed into the hardwood desk. A strange gurgly sound came from behind her lips. Svir realized she was laughing.

"You know, Hedrigs, you are the most gullible person I ever met. Correction: the second most gullible. You're a provincial, overgrown adolescent, and how you thought you could fool anyone into thinking you had ever been off the Islands is beyond me. I need that dorfox. Did you honestly believe that our encounter on Krirsarque was an *accident*? I've been studying those animals a long time. If I had you killed, I'm certain I could become Ancho's new master. Only my—high moral character prevents me from taking that course."

She smiled again. It was almost a sneer—revealing a hostility that seemed to transcend the subject at hand. "If I had known Ascuasenya could be such a nuisance, I would have kept her out of your way. Yes, I heard about your activities this afternoon. No matter. For my plans to succeed I now need some new form of leverage. Poor little Ascuasenya is perfect for my purposes."

She sat back and relaxed. "I said you were the second most gullible person in my experience. Coronadas Ascuasenya is the first. She believed me when I told her that you had already left the Barge for Bayfast. She believed me when I told her that our spies had discovered new information which you had to have to avoid disaster. She believed me when I said that with the proper credentials she could get into the Keep and warn you. And she *will* get rather far into the castle—those credentials are very good counterfeits. When she is finally discovered, the Regent's men will believe they have foiled a serious espionage attempt."

Svir stepped back from the desk, as shocked by her hostility as by what she was saying. For an instant she didn't seem human. Everything Cor had said was true. Tatja Grimm was a creature sitting at the center of an infinite complex of scheme and counterscheme, plot and counterplot—her ultimate goal beyond human understanding. Every detail of the last ten days had pushed him according to her whim. Even as she spoke now, she was trying to maneuver him into some new trap.

"Do you know what Tar Benesh does with spies, Svir Hedrigs?"

The astronomer shook his head dumbly. Grimm told him.

"And when they get done, the spy is generally burned alive," she added. "So, Svir my love, run to your cabin, get Ancho, and come back here. The briefing's going to take a while, and I want you off the Barge well before midnight."

Svir had never before wanted to kill anybody. He wanted to now—very much. This creature had imperiled the two lives he valued most. He told her so in words he had never used with a woman.

Tatja just laughed. "You may be a good astronomer, dear, but you're weak on biology. Do as I say. And don't get any ideas of taking off on your own to save Cor. You will find when I brief you that the only way you can help her is to save the *Fantasie* collection in the process."

CHAPTER 5

Six hours later, Svir Hedrigs emerged from the offices of the Tarulle executive deck and descended to the debarkation levels. He wore an old baggy suit and carried a light *balsir* cage disguised as a suitcase. Ancho sat comfortably within the cage. He wore the mysterious Clicker on his back.

The Barge had reached its pier space and was already so firmly tied in that it was difficult to tell where Barge ended and pier began. Seraph cast a bright, cheerful twilight across Bayfast. The clashing, bright colors of the city were transformed into pastels. Here and there those pastels were highlighted by yellow and green sparkles where people uncovered their evening lamps. This shimmery, glowing pattern stretched up toward the edge of the seaward cliffs and around the bay to the inland cliffs, which cut off the Monsoonal Drag and made Bayfast one of the few placid spots on The Continent at this time of year.

Svir left the Barge and walked along the waterfront. The Festival of the Ostentatious Consumption was not due to begin for another six hours, but the citizens of Bayfast were already competing with one another for the best sites along the water front from which they could watch the events on Sacrifice Island out in the bay. Svir knew he looked strange walking so seriously among the happy people. His severe costume contrasted sharply with the plaids and monochromes of the Bayfastlings. But he had his special reason for not wearing the costume Tatja had suggested.

The people of Crownesse were happy, confident, and nationalistic. Originally they had been colonists from the Chainpearl and other Archipelagates. The hardships of

The Continent had forced an optimistic dynamism on them. In the thousand years since they declared their independence from the sea, it had often been remarked that they showed the most initiative and intelligence of any people on Tu. They had developed their bureaucratic system to heights existing nowhere else in the world. Their Bureaucracy was talented, flexible and—above all—devoted to the Crown. In the last two centuries the Reaches of Crownesse had grown threefold. The country already stretched most of the way across the southern coast of The Continent, and steady inroads were being made into the Interior. But the spiritual evolution of Crownesse had ended abruptly twenty years ago, when the strange and implacable Tar Benesh appeared in the King's Court. The King had died and Tar Benesh had become the Regent Shortly after, the King's children had disappeared in a sea wreck.

Since those days twenty years before, Tar Benesh's rule had been a study in expanding tyranny. He had—with the faithful help of the Bureaucracy—transformed the open competitive spirit of the Bayfastlings into an aggressive barbarism which could worship the destruction involved in the Ostentatious Consumption, and which could desire world conquest.

Svir was walking east, toward the Keep. That enormous semi-dodecahedron loomed black over the warehouse roofs. Even the ingenious Bayfastlings had needed seventy years to build this ultimate protection for the Crown. Nothing short of a year-long artillery bombardment could breach that artificial mountain—and the Keep had plenty of its own armament. Just ventilating the structure required the services of twenty draft animals.

Svir stopped before he reached the two-hundred-foot open space surrounding the Keep. He slipped into the entranceway of a closed shop and covertly inspected the castle port through which he must pass. Once more the horrible fear rose in him, making his every movement slow and clumsy. He was going to die. The whole plan was so complicated, and depended so heavily on Ancho and the tenuous information Tatja had about the inside of the Keep. But he knew he wasn't going to back out. Tatja had discovered the one motive strong enough to make him take any risk. It had worked with Cor and now it was working with him.

A figure dressed in the uniform of a Guard captain walked across the open area toward the port. That was the signal to begin. The "captain" was a Tarulle agent whose job it was to tip the Guardsmen at the door to look sharp since the Crown's Inspector General was expected momentarily. In truth, the Crown's IG was supposed to visit the Keep at this time, but he was being detained by other Tarulle agents. In any case the two Guardsmen at the door should now be prepared to assume that the next authority figure they saw was the Inspector General.

Svir fumbled the suitcase open and lifted Ancho out. The animal responded nervously to the human's obvious anxiety. Svir tried to reassure him. As per instructions he depressed the tiny button on the side of the box strapped to Ancho's back. The contraption immediately began making a *click-clock-click* sound.

What if the device were a bomb hooked up to a clock, timed to blow up after they were within the Keep? He debated for a moment whether to rip the machine off Ancho's back. But there was no explosive which could possibly be fitted into a package this small and still do any damage to the castle. Tatja had no motive for tagging him with a clock bomb. And since his survival was necessary for the salvation of the *Fantasie* collection, the device probably had some beneficial—though certainly mysterious—role.

He stood up, put the dorfox on his shoulder, and petted him. The animal began radiating immediately. His first target was a middle-aged merchant—one of the few people who were not yet at the waterfront. As the man passed Svir and Ancho, his eyes widened and he performed the nodding bow reserved for members of the Bureaucracy. Svir smiled and walked onto the open area before the Keep. In some peculiar way, when Ancho used the effect on others, it made Svir feel confident, competent. And this feeling of authority actually seemed to feed back to the animal, making him perform even more effectively. Svir strolled briskly across the grassy plain.

The two Guardsmen came rigidly to attention as he approached. One of them saluted. Svir offhandedly returned the salute. He passed his credentials to the Guardsman. At the same time he spoke the ritual words. "The Crown's agent to inventory the Prizes."

The senior Guardsman looked up from the papers. "Very good, sir." Both men wore ridiculously ornamented dress uniforms, but there was nothing ornamental about their weapons. In a single glance, the Guardsman gave Svir a thorough once-over. His alert and active mind checked for the minor details that would give an impostor away. Unfortunately for the Guardsman, his own mind made him see the details he was looking for. If questioned later, both Guards would swear they saw the Crown's Inspector General enter the building, not Svir Hedrigs.

The fellow returned Svir his papers and turned to an inconspicuous speaking tube that emerged from the black stone of the castle wall. Except for the words "Inspector General," Svir couldn't hear what was said. But that was enough. He had passed the second hurdle. At each checkpoint, the word would be passed back as to who he was supposed to be. With a greased sliding sound, a thirty-ton cube of stone lifted into the ceiling of the entrance. Beyond was darkness.

Svir walked in, striving not to look up at the mass of stone above him, or back at the colorful city which would soon be blocked from his view. The stone cube slid smoothly down. He stood in the dark for almost five seconds. Ancho chirped nervously, and the device on his back continued to *clock-click-clock*. He rubbed Ancho's neck, and the little dorfox began radiating again. None too soon. A second block of stone was lifting. Algae-generated light flooded the chamber. He stepped into the hallway revealed and handed his papers to the Guardsmen standing there. Two of them were right by the entrance, while a third stood on a crenelated balcony near the ceiling. All three were dressed in loose, comfortable suits of Bureaucratic black. They weren't nearly as formal as the fellows outside, but they showed obvious respect—and they were just as alert and competent. Svir's identity was passed by speaking tube to the next checkpoint.

He walked on confidently. The hall was well lighted and ventilated—even though it was within a mass of stone almost six hundred feet high. In some places the cold black stone was covered by wood paneling and cabinets filled with the Arms of Early Kings. He passed through three more checkpoints, each with its own door system. Whenever he had a choice of routes he took the middle one—he was following a radius straight to the center of the Keep, to the Crown Room vault. Some of the outer passages were almost crowded. Bureaucrats were making final arrangements for the evening's events. Svir walked aloof from these groups, and hoped that none of them compared notes on exactly who they thought he was. As he approached the center, however, there were fewer and fewer people. Besides the Guards, he encountered only an occasional very-high-ranking Bureaucrat.

Here the identification procedures became more complex. The walls were uniformly paneled and the floors heavily carpeted. Svir wondered at this strange luxuriousness in the most secret part of the Keep. Besides the usual paintings and displays, there were small glass windows at regular intervals. Beyond that glass, Svir could see only darkness. Probably there was someone back there watching what went on—guarding the guards. Svir was suddenly very glad that Tatja had had Ancho practice at deluding hidden observers. Now he knew the reason for the luxurious trappings. Besides hiding the observation posts, they probably concealed a variety of weapons and deadfalls.

Finally he reached the last checkpoint—the doorway to the Crown Room itself. It was conceivable that at this moment only the Inspector General and Tar Benesh himself had authority to enter that storeroom of the nation's greatest treasures and most secret documents. Here the clearance process was especially difficult. For a few uncomfortable moments, Svir thought they were going to take his fingerprints and run a comparison right there. Would the illusion extend to fingerprints? But apparently that procedure was used in special cases only, and Svir was not subjected to it.

As they opened the outer vault door, he casually turned to the officer in charge. "Captain, I have instructions to move some of the Prizes out to Sacrifice Island right away. I'd like to have a couple of squads ready when I finish the general inventory."

"Very good, sir," she answered. "We have about twenty people with the proper clearance for just that job. I can have them here in fifteen minutes." She handed Svir an algae lamp. "Don't forget this, sir."

"Why, thanks." He accepted the lamp uncertainly. "If everything's in order, my inventory should take about forty minutes—if not, it could be longer." *A lot longer,* he thought to himself.

He turned and walked quickly into the lock area between the double doors. The outer door slid shut, the inner door lifted open, and he stepped into the Crown Room.

The vault was a disappointment. The room was large and without ornamentation. Svir's lamp provided the only illumination. Over all hung a musty smell, which the tiny vault ventilator shafts could not dissipate. The treasures were not heaped in some spectacular pile, but were neatly catalogued on racks that filled most of the room. Each object had its own classification tag. A row of cabinets along one wall housed the personal records of the Royal Family. Svir walked along the racks. (He almost didn't notice the Crown Jewels and the 930-carat Shamerest-cut diamond; in the dim light everything looked dull.) Finally he reached the red-tag area—the prime sacrifices for the Festival.

And there it was—the *Fantasie* collection. Its sheer bulk was impressive. The ten thousand volumes were stacked on seven close-set racks. The entire mass rested on a dolly for easy handling. Obviously Benesh thought of *Fantasie* as an article of portable wealth rather than a source of philosophical and romantic pleasure. But—as Tatja so cynically pointed out—that massive collection was also the vehicle of Cor's salvation. Even in this dim light, he could read some of the binding titles. Why, there was the last *obra* of Ti Liso's time-travel series! For the last three centuries, the Chainpearl experts had been trying to find that issue. The series had been illustrated by Inmar Ellis—probably the greatest artist of all time. Svir noticed all this in passing. No matter how valuable this collection, its physical dimensions were much more important to him now. There was indeed enough room between the third and fourth racks to hide a human body.

Now he had to find the correct passage to the prison

tier. If Tatja had lied about that . . . But if she lied, then she couldn't possibly get the collection. Not by Svir's efforts, anyway.

The vault doors were so well constructed that Svir did not notice that he had been discovered until the inner door lifted and he heard the raging voice of—

Tar Benesh.

The Regent advanced into the room. A look of astounded shock came to his face as he saw Svir. Svir wondered briefly what authority figure the dictator saw in Ancho's illusion.

Benesh was less than five feet tall. He weighed more than two hundred pounds. Once that weight had been slab-like muscle, but now he was as soft as the velvet and flutter-feather costume he wore.

He shakily raised his arm and pointed at Svir. "Take that—man," he choked. The black-uniformed Guardsmen swarmed toward Svir, their momentary confusion replaced by cool professionalism. Svir felt only confidence as they approached. He was in trouble, true, but he could work his way out of it.

The confidence vanished. As the Guardsmen grabbed him, Svir collapsed into the quivering apathy of total fear. He felt a burning needle thrust into the base of his neck, and simultaneously his entire body became a single charley horse. He couldn't move, he could hardly breath, and what he saw and heard seemed to be far away, observed through a curtain of pain. He felt his person being searched, and dimly heard Benesh say, "A dorfox, that's the creature you saw."

"But M'Lord Regent, that's a mythological creature."

"Obviously not! Search the Crown Room." An unprecedented order. "No one enters or leaves this vault till we find—" He paused, realizing that this was impractical. It would tie up the Guard situation in the whole Keep. "No, forget that. But I want that creature, and I want it alive." There was a lustfulness in his voice. "Check everyone and everything that passes through these doors."

Svir felt himself picked up, moved swiftly toward the door. And of all the humans in the room, he was the only one who noticed the dorfox seated on the shoulder of Tar Benesh.

As they rushed him through the Keep passageways, Svir vaguely wondered what had given him away—though he really didn't care now. Nothing could save Cor and himself. And soon this paralysis would be replaced by the ultimate agony of interrogation.

Finally his captors stopped. There was a dull creaking sound. Then he was sailing through the air. His hip struck the hard stone floor, contributing an extra fire to his general pain. His head and shoulders were resting in a pile of straw. He smelled rot and blood. The heavy door swung shut and he was in darkness.

There was a shuffling sound, and someone was holding him. Cor! She pressed her body tight against his and whispered in his ear what seemed a complete irrelevancy. "I'm so sorry, Svir! I tried to warn you but they got me." She was silent for a second, waiting for some response. He longed to put his arms around her. "Svir?" she whispered. "Are you all right? Svir!" But he was so thoroughly paralyzed he couldn't even croak.

CHAPTER 6

"—realize we're sitting beneath the Keep artillery. To get out, we'd have to go around the peninsula past the entrance guns. And now you want me to send twenty people on a diversionary raid! If Benesh ever connects us with this scheme, we'll be blown out of the water—if we're lucky!" Kederichi Maccioso slammed his broad fist down on Tatja's desk, jarring her aluminum drinking carafe half an inch into the air.

"Relax, Ked, we aren't suspected of anything yet. It's still a state secret that the collection is one of the sacrifices. There's—" She broke off and motioned Maccioso to be silent. Even over the thrumming crowd sounds outside, they could both hear a scratching against the office window.

Tatja Grimm pushed the window open and pulled a shivering, croaking Ancho into the room. She held him close and comforted him with low, gentle sounds. Maccioso sat down abruptly and stared at them, shocked.

"The . . . dorfox wouldn't come back alone unless Hedrigs had been taken," he stuttered.

Tatja smiled. "That's right. Svir never had a chance—though he lasted longer than I thought he would."

"But this means Benesh knows. We've got to get a—" Then he seemed to realize what Tatja had just said. "*What?* You knew all along he would fail?" His voice rose to an astonishing volume, rattled the window. "We're all going to die because of you, you—"

"Shut up, Ked," Tatja said pleasantly. "You're disturbing Ancho. Do you really think I would do anything to jeopardize my own life?" She set Ancho on her desk. "You know," she said with apparent irrelevance, "I've studied dorfoxes. If they were just a little smarter or a little more mobile, they could take over the world. As it is, though, I can manipulate them. With Hedrigs out of the way, I think Ancho will accept me as his new master." She undid the Clicker and set it carefully on her desk. "Hand me that bottle of lacquer, will you?" She accepted the bottle and screwed an atomizer onto its cap. Then she inserted the nozzle into the Clicker's keyhole and puffed the volatile lacquer into the box. In spite of himself, Kederichi Maccioso leaned over the table to watch this mysterious ritual. Ancho moved over to the corner of the table and munched the *klig* leaves that Tatja had thoughtfully provided.

"That should fix it." She undid the hidden catches and lifted the top off the box. "You know that picturemaker we've been using in our latest issues? I've made some refinements on the invention."

Maccioso looked at the machine's innards. It resembled only vaguely the picturemaker that Tarulle used. In that device, light was focused on a special cellulose plate coated with very fine algae powder. Wherever light fell on the plate, the cellulose became charged and repelled the greenish powder from its surface. If the plate were properly coated with lacquer, a permanent picture resulted.

Tatja pointed. "See, this clock movement pulls the reel of cellulose tape through the central area. Once every two seconds, this shutter takes an exposure. On alternate seconds, the shutter on the other side of the box takes a picture. So we now have a pictorial record covering nearly three hundred degrees. A picture every second for nearly ten minutes." She pulled the reel out of the Clicker and began to examine it under a large magnifying glass. Maccioso had a clear, though distorted, view of the pictures through the same lens.

The first thirty pictures covered Svir's approach to the Keep. Every other pitcture was reversed, since it had been made on the opposite side of the cellulose. In spite of this and the fact that the pictures were considerably less clear then ones made with simpler, one-shot devices, the sequence gave Maccioso the unreal sensation that he was sitting on Svir's shoulder. On every second frame, Svir's head blocked out part of the picture.

Tatja carefully inspected each picture, but it was obvious that she didn't expect anything strange this early in the sequence. She became increasingly excited as the pictures showed the interior of the Keep. Here the exposure she had chosen was much more effective and the pictures sharper. "See, that paneling and those paintings—they weren't in any of the reports. And here, I'll bet this is what snagged dear Hedrigs."

Maccioso squinted at the tiny picture. It looked no different than the three or four previous. Then Tatja pointed out the rectangular patch of darkness on the passage wall. "That's not a painting. It's some kind of window. My guess is that the Guards have heard of the poison gases developed in the Sutherseas. That little window is one end of a periscope, and the observer is in another room, protected from the gas—and apparently beyond Ancho's range." They looked at the rest of the pictures, but most were badly fogged. As the exposures had been made, more and more algae powder had been sent into a suspension in the Clicker. An equilibrium state had been reached—where as much green was being deposited as was being dissipated by the exposures. Those last pictures showed vague green blurs. They saw something of the interior of the Crown Room. And in one of the pictures, Tatja claimed she saw a group of men.

She set the film aside and picked up a compass. "We discovered that Ancho can broadcast through almost twenty feet of porphyry." She made some rapid measurements of relative sizes on the film. "That periscope window is about three inches by three." She sat back and her eyes unfocused for a moment. "Now assuming their optics are no better than elsewhere, that periscope can't have a resolution higher than half an inch." She looked up and flashed Maccioso a dazzling smile. "I'm all set! Svir has served his purpose."

Tatja got up and began to take her clothes off. Maccioso stood up too. He was a big man, an experienced man, a leader. But he appeared to be none of these now. His face bore a peculiar mixture of hatred, surprise, and confusion. Once he loved this woman. As Tatja laid her shirt on the chair, he reached out a huge hand, grabbed her by the shoulder, drew her face close to his.

"You never intended this plan to save *Fantasie,* did you?"

Tatja just shrugged, "You know the saying, Ked. 'Things are not as they seem.' "

"What are you after then, damn you?" He shook her violently, but received no answer. "Well, if you think I'm going to risk any more Tarulle people for your pleasure, you're crazy."

"Poor Ked," Tatja said gently. Her hand moved softly up his arm, found a nerve in his elbow. As he jerked back, she slipped from his hold. "I see that I've driven you almost beyond logic and self-interest. Almost." She reached into an alcove and drew out a complete set of black armor. The Crown's Inspector General was about her height, but the armor had been designed for a male. In places it chafed tight, but she managed to get it on.

She slipped the épée into its sheath and picked Ancho up from the desk. At the door she turned back to face Maccioso. "But I know you will go through with that attack. You know that whatever my plan is, it's the only chance you have of getting out of this alive, now that Benesh has Ascuasenya and Hedrigs. Right?"

Kederichi Maccioso glowered at her for a moment, then slowly nodded his head, defeated. "That's right, you . . . bitch."

Seraph was in its last quarter, and the evening wake period was ending. Nearly a million people—the entire population of the capital—were crowded along the water's edge. In the waning blue light the crowd was a mosaic carpet covering the streets and stretching up over the roofs of the lower buildings. The Festival was at its noisiest as the Bayfastlings cheered the first sacrifices being towed into the bay. These were the secondary sacrifices—the appetizers. The tiny barges formed a continuous train out to Sacrifice Island. Each barge was stacked high with worked jade, optical devices, paintings. Hanging from the stern of each barge, an algae-water sphere lit the sacrifices.

A twisted smile crossed Tatja's lips as she regarded the scene.

She descended to one of the sub-pier passageways

reserved for official use, and five minutes later emerged on the city side of the crowd. Here were the stragglers, the individuals without initiative enough to push into the crowd. She petted Ancho, spoke quietly to him. This was a critical test. According to theory, Ancho should accept her as his new master, but Tatja had to be sure. She couldn't tell whether he was radiating or not. Certainly the signal was having no effect on her. Then she noticed that people came to attention as she walked past. Good Ancho.

She reached the Keep without incident. The Guardsmen looked her over very carefully, this being the second Inspector General they had seen that day. But they let her through. As she stood in the darkness between the two doors, she moved the dorfox to her waist. The armor plates gave him good purchase, and now he was below the view of the periscopes.

As she came to the doors of the Crown Room, Tatja spoke in a low, masculine voice to fool any listening devices. Even with her visor up, she knew that wearing the IG's armor would deceive the hidden observers. And of course the Guardsmen in the hall didn't have a chance. With Ancho's help, even her fingerprints passed inspection.

Once in the Crown Room she moved quickly to the Royal records. She lifted out the drawer she wanted, thumbed through it, and pulled out a single sheet of vellum. Good. It was the same form as had been publicly displayed at the Assignation of the Regency. From her pouch she drew a seemingly identical paper, smudges and all, and slipped it into the file.

Then she left, ignoring the puzzled Guards. They had expected the IG to supervise the removal of the prizes.

Tatja found the stairway to the Conciliar Facet unguarded. This was unexpected good fortune. Perhaps Maccioso's diversion had been more effective than she had planned.

She removed the black resin armor and set the outfit on one of the display racks which lined the base of the stairwell. This was the most perilous part of her plan. If she were discovered in the next three or four minutes, there'd be real trouble. From a gray cloth pouch she drew a white dress and jeweled sandals. She slipped them on, put Ancho on her shoulder, and ran up the stairs. This stairway wasn't often used, since it was a single spiral ascending six hundred feet. Most people preferred to go by stages. Even so, Tatja kept the heavy épée. Except for that épée, and the dorfox clutching her shoulder, she might have been an Island girl at a communion picnic.

She took the steps three at a time, so fast that she had to lean toward the center of the spiral in order to keep her balance. When she had first conceived this scheme, she had spent three years in Bayfast studying the people and especially the Keep. Tar Benesh had created the Festival of the Ostentatious Consumption in order to draw attention from a much more solemn event that took place every five years at the same time. The top people in the Bureaucracy were scrupulously honest, but if she were even five minutes late, she would have to wait five years—or possibly forever. Taking the back way should save her from Benesh's Special Men, but if she were wrong about the Bureaucratic esprit of the rest, then she would die—though death could make her failure no worse. If she couldn't succeed, life wasn't worth living.

Tatja took the six-hundred-foot stairway in a single sprint. At the top of that long flight was an entrance to the Conciliar Facet, the pentagonal amphitheater on the very top of the enormous dodecahedron that was the Keep. Beyond this next door was the final test. She slid the door open and crept out onto the uppermost tier of the amphitheater. There was a faint cool breeze, and Seraph-blue covered everything. From the city came crowd sounds.

Less than a third of the seats in the Facet were filled, and those were down in the center, by the podium and reading lamp. Virtually everyone present was dressed in Bureaucratic black. An important exception was the gross and colorful bulk of Tar Benesh, sitting in the first row before the podium.

Tatja glanced around the Facet. Maccioso's diversion must have worked. Few of the Guards appeared to be Benesh's bully boys. There were only fifteen or twenty armed men present. Of course one of them might still be rotten, but that was a chance she must take. She noticed one man just five feet from her hiding place. The fellow leaned unprofessionally against the edge of the tier, blocking her entrance. She reversed the hilt of the épée and moved swiftly forward, ramming the pommel into the base of the man's neck. He collapsed quietly into her arms. She dragged him back, at the same time watching for signs that someone below had noticed the incident.

The speaker's voice came clearly to her. She knew there were about five minutes until the ceremony reached its critical point. She looked at her épée. It was no longer an asset. Without putting herself in silhouette, she reached up and slid the weapon over the battlement. There came a faint sound of scrape and clatter as the épée slid slowly down the side of the hundred-foot facet. Tatja sat Ancho on the edge of the tier and petted him. They waited.

In the center of the amphitheater, the ceremony was nearing its end. On the podium stood the Lord High Minister to the Crown—the highest Bureaucratic officer of Crownesse. The man was old, but his body was lean, and his voice was clear and strong as he read from the curling parchment. He had the air of a man who is for the thousandth time repeating a fervent and sincere prayer, a prayer that has so often been fruitless that it has almost become perfunctory.

"And so in the Year of the Discovery nine hundred and seven did the Crown Prince Evard II and his sister, Princess Marget, take themselves aboard the Royal Yacht *Avante* to tour the western reaches of their Dominions.

"And on the fifth day of their voyage a great storm sent their yacht upon the Rocks of the South—for so we have the word of the ship's captain and those crewmen who survived the tragedy."

Tatja stood up slowly, out of their view. She fluffed out her full skirt and waited quietly for the moment that would come.

"The Royal Children were never found. So it is that the Regent continues to govern in their stead until such time as our rulers are recovered. On this twenty-fifth anniversary of that storm, and by order of the Regent, I ask that anyone with knowledge of the Royal Family step forth." The Lord High Minister glanced about moodily. The ceremony was almost a legal fiction. It had been fifteen years since anyone had dared Tar Benesh's revenge with a story of the lost children. It is not surprising that the Minister almost fell off the stand when a clear, vibrant voice answered his call.

"I, Marget of Sandros, do claim the Crown and my Dominions." Tatja stood boldly on the uppermost tier, her arms akimbo. Behind her, and invisible to those below, sat a small animal with large ears. The startled Bureaucrats stared at Tatja, the beautiful woman who had turned a ceremony into a coup. Then their eyes turned to the Regent. How would he accept this challenge? The gaily dressed dictator advanced six ominous steps toward Tatja. His pale eyes reflected hatred and complete disbelief. For twenty years he had ruled the most powerful country on Tu—and now a female was challenging him at the very center of his power. Benesh gestured angrily to the Guardsmen—the sleek professionals with thousands of hours of target and tactical experience, the deadliest individuals in the world.

"Kill the impostor," he ordered.

CHAPTER 7

When they came, Svir was ready.

He and Cor had lain quietly in the darkness, telling each other their stories in frightened whispers. As Cor massaged the numbness from his arms, Svir told her of his one backstop against Tatja's treachery. Tounse—who hated Tatja as much as Svir did—had provided him with five pounds of Michelle-Rasche powder. Now that powder lay in the heavy fiber weave of his clothing.

"It's perfectly safe until the cloth gets twisted into a constricted volume," he whispered to Cor. "But then almost any extra friction will set it off."

He struggled out of his overjacket. Cor helped him wedge the fabric into the door crack. Though only a small portion of the jacket could be jammed in, it would be enough to set off the rest of the powder. Then they retreated to the far corner of the cell. There was nothing more they could do. He hadn't said so to Cor, but the best they could hope for was a quick death. If they weren't killed in the explosion or by the Guards—then the next stop was the torture chambers. Their present cell was a carefully contrived filth-pit, designed to prepare prisoners psychologically for what was to come. Somehow the prospect of torture and death no longer provoked absolute terror in him. Cor was the reason. He wanted to hide his fear from her—and to protect her from her own fears.

He put his arm around Cor's waist and drew her to him. "You came out here to save me, Cor."

"You did the same for me, Svir."

"I'd do it all over again."

Her reply was clear and firm. "I, too."

When they came, there was plenty of warning. It sounded like a whole squad. The heavy footsteps stopped, and when they began again, it sounded like only two or three men. Svir and Cor slid under the filthy straw. The footsteps stopped at the door. Svir heard the key turn, but he never heard the door open. For that matter, he never actually *heard* the explosion. He felt it through his whole body. The floor rose up and smashed him.

He forced himself to his feet, and pulled Cor up. The doorway was a dim patch of light through the dust and vapor that the explosion had driven into the air. They gasped futilely and ran toward the opening. Svir was aware of blood flowing down his jaw from his ear

The blast had destroyed the bottom hinges on the door and blown the whole mass into the ceiling. In the hallway lay the two Guardsmen. Both were alive, but in much worse shape than the prisoners. One, with a severe scalp cut, tried ineffectually to wipe the blood from his eyes. Svir and Cor stepped over them and ran down the hall. Then they saw the men at the end of the passage—the back-up section. The two prisoners came to a sudden halt and started to turn in the other direction.

A Guardsman smiled faintly and twisted a lever mounted in the wall. A weighted net fell from the ceiling onto the two escapees. As the Guard approached, Svir lashed out at his legs, hoping to provoke lethal retaliation. The Guard easily avoided the extended hand, and grabbed it with his own. "You know, fella, for someone whose life we're supposed to protect, you're making things damn difficult."

Svir looked back blankly. He couldn't make sense of the words spoken. The net was removed, and the Guards marched Svir and Cor down the hall. The couple looked at each other in complete confusion. They weren't even treated to the paralysis the Guards had used before. It was a long uphill walk, and the Guards had to help Cor the last part. Svir wondered if he had gone crazy with fear and was seeing only what he hoped to see. They came to the final door. The Guard captain went through. They could hear him through the open doorway.

"Marget, the individuals you requested are here."

"Fine," came a familiar voice. "Send them out. I want to talk to them alone."

"Begging your pardon, Marget, but they have repeatedly offered us violence. We could not guarantee the safety of your person if you interview them alone."

"Mister, I told you what I wanted." The voice took a tone that brooked no argument. "Now jump!"

"Yes, Marget, immediately!" The captain appeared at the door. He gestured courteously to Svir and Cor. "Sir and Madam, you have been granted an interview with the Queen."

"The—*Queen?*" Cor asked incredulously. She got no answer. They were pushed past the door and found themselves standing on the top tier of the Conciliar Facet. By the light of waning Seraph they saw a beautiful girl in a full-skirted dress.

Tatja turned to them. "You two look like hell," she said.

Svir started angrily toward her. All his fright and pain was transformed into hate for this monster who pretended to be human. There was a scuttling sound on the floor, then a tugging at Svir's clothing. A soft wet nose nuzzled his neck. Ancho! Svir's hands reached up and petted the trembling animal.

"Marget?" asked Cor. "Queen? Really are you the Lost Princess of Crownesse?"

"Since you were in on part of the scheme, I suppose you might as well know the truth. You can't do anything about it. I was no more Marget of Sandros than you. But now I am incontrovertibly the Queen. My fingerprints match those of the Princess which are kept in the Crown Room. You should have seen the look on Benesh's face when the Lord High Minister announced that I was heir to the Crown. The Regent had the Royal Children murdered twenty years ago. The job was bobbled and he couldn't produce bodies that would pass an autopsy. He *knew* I was a fraud but there was no way he could prove it without revealing that he was guilty of regicide."

Svir looked out over the curving dome of the Keep toward the city. The crowd sounds came clear and faint through the air. The crowd had moved away from the waterfront. There would be no sacrifices tonight—the people had been told that the Crown had been claimed. Crownesse had a Queen. That called for the largest of festivals, a celebration that would go on for many days.

Svir turned to Tatja Grimm. "You had to lie and cheat and steal and—probably—murder to do it, but you certainly got what you wanted. You control the most powerful country in the world. I've wondered so many times what could make you as vicious as you are. Now I know. The hidden motive that mystified me so much was simple megalomania. Female 'Tar Benesh' has taken over from male. Is this the end of your appetites," he said, putting as much derision and hate into his voice as he could, "or will you one day rule all Tu?"

Tatja smiled at Cor and Svir—the same scornful, bitter smile they had seen so often before. "You never were very bright, were you, Svir? It's possible that I'll take over the world. As a matter of fact, I probably will. It will be a byproduct of my other plans. I chose Crownesse very carefully. The country has immense physical resources. If there are large heavy-metal deposits anywhere, they are in Crownesse. The government is talented and dedicated. Most administrative posts are awarded on the basis of civil service tests. And the entire Bureaucracy is fanatically dedicated to one person—the legal holder of the Crown. They served Tar Benesh and his evil for twenty years, and they will serve me just as faithfully. I will not be bothered with coups and elections, as I might if I took over one of the archipelagates.

"We've reached a very critical point in the development of civilization—in case you don't realize it. In the past century there have been a number of really basic scientific discoveries made in all parts of the world. The pharmacists of the Tsanart Islands have developed drugs which control most of the major diseases. A physicist in the Osterlai Archipelagate developed that picturemaker we use. All over the world, revolutionary advances are being made. Sometimes I think that organizations like Tarulle are responsible for this. For centuries they spread ideas from island to island until finally scientists stopped thinking of them as fantasy and actually invented what writers described. I'm making a gift of that *Fantasie* collection to Tarulle, by the way."

"That's big of you," snapped Svir.

Tatja ignored him. "All these inventions and techniques are going to have effects far beyond what is obvious. Just think what that picturemaker will do for parallax astronomy. You'll be able to make pictures of all observations. If these inventions were brought together and worked over intensively, the changes would be even more spectacular. But you people out in the islands are too lazy to do that. The people of Crownesse are not. They've had to work awfully hard just to stay alive here on The Continent. They will take your inventions and use them and develop more inventions—until they control the entire planet."

She looked up into the sky, at Seraph and the bright star Prok. "You know, there is a legend among the Wildmen at the center of The Continent. The legend says that man originally came from the stars, that he landed on The Continent and lost his magical arts to the storm and the wind. Sounds like a *Fantasie* story, doesn't it? But in the last five years I've had access to just about every major library in the world. Taken all together, I see a tenuous pattern: it's quite possible that we have been *visited* several times in the last thousand years, at multiples of one hundred seventeen years. Imagine—if this is true, then the races of man may live among the stars, their empires so vast that they can 'lose' whole planetary systems. Perhaps they colonized Seraph at the same time as Tu. We are not alone."

As she spoke, Tatja's voice changed, lost its authority and its spite. Now she spoke softly, sadly. Her shoulders slumped slightly. For a moment she wasn't the master of all events, but a young girl, very much alone, and very lonely. "No, Svir, ruling this world does not interest me, except for one thing. I've never found anyone I can talk to, anyone who can understand the things I often want to say. When I call you stupid—I mean it, even though you're of above-average intelligence, and even though I just say it to make you angry."

She turned to look at Svir and Cor. Her eyes were soft, and her lower lip almost trembled. Her vast intelligence had crippled her, just as surely as if she had had no arms. In blunt point of fact, there was no person on Tu who was her equal. Svir suddenly understood the meaning of her scornful, hostile smile. It was the bitter, hopeless envy of a woman seeing well-adjusted people all around her and not being one herself.

"And that is why I am going to turn this world upside down, and regain the ancient arts that mythology said we once had. For somewhere in this universe there *must* be what I need most . . . a man."

The fallen goddess turned away from the parapet and the gay crowds. She didn't look up as she walked slowly away.

PART II

CHAPTER 8

The Astronomer Royal was all wet. At Bayfast the Waterfall lasted more than thirty days—nearly the quarter part of a year. For the last twenty-eight days and nights it had rained without pause. Many of the city's troughed streets were filled with swift-moving water. Behind all sounds was the rumbly hum of myriad droplets striking stone and wood and water. After four years, the Astronomer Royal was still not accustomed to the monsoon climate of the Continent. At the back of his mind was the irrational thought that when the rain stopped, Seraph might be washed from the sky.

Svir briefly considered returning to his carriage. It wasn't worth it; he was already too wet. By the Bayfast logic, if the rain is warm—why stay dry? With a mixture of irritation and envy, he watched the Guardsmen on the pier. They appeared to enjoy being wet to the skin. They wore their slack uniforms with a cockiness that indicated they thought being soaked was the height of fashion—which at this time and place it was.

His carriage was parked on the roadway near the pier. The Guards were stationed at the root of the stone pier. Behind the roadway were the naval warehouses, constructed of marble bricks and rock paste. The quarries on the inland cliffs across the bay seemed inexhaustible, and the Crown's Men had used them to build one of the most peculiar and beautiful warehouse districts in the world. Architects claimed that the naval portion of the port could survive artillery attack and was absolutely nonflammable. Svir wasn't so sure about the first claim, but during the Waterfall he was certain no fire could be started outside the warehouses. The pier had an inch of water on it even though it was more than ten feet above the cratered water of the bay.

Perhaps he should have stayed in the dryrooms of the Keep. But as Astronomer Royal, he felt that this was a job which could not be delegated. The fastboat they were expecting was to bring the most recent reports from the Doomsday observatory, four thousand miles northward along the coast of The Continent and more than twenty nine thousand feet above sea level—above the monsoonal precipitation. During the Waterfall, the Doomsdaymen were the most important source of astronomical information the Crown possessed. Svir's most important job was to collect and arrange these reports for Marget's consideration. And since Marget really needed no help in the interpretation of astronomical data, the Astronomer Royal frequently felt superfluous. At least it felt important to come down here to the most restricted area of the naval district and welcome a fastboat from a war zone.

In fact, thought Svir as he glanced about at the people on the dock, he was nominally the highest ranking man on the pier. The only other first-level officer was a vice-admiral from naval intelligence. The single broad gray band on Svir's sleeve identified him as a high minister. He generally tried to conceal the tiny crown above that band, since the crown indicated he was an appointee rather than a civil service man.

The Astronomer Royal squished unhappily across the pier to the admiral. The navy man saluted. "Good day, m'lord."

Svir supressed some sarcasm as he noticed there was no humor in the admiral's blue eyes. "I was told the fastboat would arrive by twenty-five hours."

"That's right, sir. But unless the wind is steady, the hydrofoils are useless and the boat is as slow as any other."

Svir didn't point out that except during the Turnabouts, the Monsoonal Drag always blew right for high-speed travel along the coast. The admiral seemed worried enough. Svir casually covered the crown on his left sleeve with his right hand. Who would have guessed four years ago that one day the most powerful men of the most powerful country in the world would address him as their superior? Even more fantastic—who would have thought four years ago that he would some day be married to anyone as wonderful as Coronadas Ascuasenya? Ever since that night in Krirsarque, his life had been like the story of the Little Sailmaker: success piled upon fantastic success.

But he did not delude himself. He was riding the bow-wave of what was probably the most spectacular success story in the history of man: the career of Marget, Queen of Crownesse, née Tatja Grimm. Tatja's rise to power had been miraculous, but her reputation since had been still more colorful. Many of her national projects seemed pointless, extravagant, halfwitted. But a halfwit she was not. For every person who despised her, there were now three who worshiped her. And that ratio was improving. Her fastboat program had at first seemed ridiculous. Who wants to know what's happening on the other side of the world within twenty days of the event? But that program had already repaid itself five times over. With a comparatively instantaneous picture of the world's markets, Crownesse merchants had achieved even greater dominance throughout Tu. This and other successes gave people excuse to overlook her other projects. As far as Svir knew, there were only two people besides Tatja who knew her ultimate purpose—and he was one of those two. He sometimes wondered if his present post were not intended to pay for his silence. Marget was merciful.

Svir glanced at the admiral, and wondered what that fellow's solution to the Marget Mystery might be. The naval officer was staring across the bay at the north inland cliffs. High in those hills was the signaling mosaic that relayed messages from the seaward cliffs—the Somnai. Through the rain, Svir could barely make out the shifting patterns of orange and blue on the mosaic. "That's it, sir!" the admiral spoke. "The Somnai batteries have spotted the fastboat. . . . It's entering the bay right now." His relief was plain. The troops the Crown had sent north to put down the rebellion had been lightly equipped. It had been Marget's idea to use fastboats to transport two thousand troops for a surprise pincer attack in cooperation with the Loyalist army south of the Rebels. This insurrection was the only blot on the Queen's record. Sixty days earlier, fastboats from the North had begun to report rumors that asserted that she was an impostor and that her accession had been accomplished by fraud. This claim was especially disturbing because it was true. But it was surprising because nearly three and a half years had passed since the accession, and except for the deposed Tar Benesh, no one had protested. (Svir suspected, though, that some of the higher members of the Bureaucracy had guessed the truth.) Recently these rumors had blossomed into an armed insurrection. And Marget's shock troops had departed just ten days ago. The returning fastboat would bring news of the battle as well as the astronomical reports that Svir was interested in.

A half-hour passed. The fastboat appeared in the rain-grayed distance. The bay was comparatively windless, and the boat's crew was rowing it slowly toward the pier.

Svir shook his sleeves, hoping to free the sticky linen from his skin. He had about reached his limit for this drowned-rat feeling. He squinted to get a clearer view of the fastboat. Its boom masts were in the vertical position and its sails were, of course, reefed—but there was something strange about its appearance, nevertheless. Then he realized that the boat's port side had only three masts while the starboard had four. He could see the stub of the amputated boom still hanging in the extended position. The boat listed slightly to port.

He pointed to the boat. "Admiral, that boat's been shot up."

The older man stared for a few seconds. Then he glanced back at the Astronomer Royal, noticed the crown on Svir's sleeve. "So it has." Apparently the admiral reserved "sir" and "m'lord" for his real superiors—civil service people. He turned and walked quickly away toward the end of the pier. Svir followed.

Several large holes were visible in the fastboat's hull,

barely above the water line. A suspicious brown stain covered portions of the boat's streamlined foredeck. As the Guardsmen made way for Svir, he moved forward to the edge of the pier. Now he was only a yard from the little craft. A strange sickly smell came from below decks. He looked across at the sailors. They were busy making the boat secure. They moved quickly, efficiently, but their faces were strained and their eyes fixed.

Finally the main hatch opened and the commanding officer appeared on deck. His uniform was as sharp as fatigue uniforms ever are, but his arm was in a sling and the left side of his face was a smear of medicant and blood. Following close behind him came a sailor carrying the heavywood strongbox that was the fastboat's cargo—the reports from Upcoast, from the war zone.

Svir felt a bit nauseated. He stepped to the edge of the pier to give the wounded man a hand up. The fellow glanced at the gray band on his sleeve, came to attention and saluted.

"Lieutenant Mörl reports return Fastboat One Nineteen, m'lord," he recited.

"My God, man, what happened?" Behind him, Svir felt the admiral trying to maneuver him away from the edge of the pier. High minister or not, Svir had just committed a substantial breach of protocol—if not security—by asking for an oral report at this time. But the wounded Lieutenant Mörl was too exhausted to notice much beyond the rank on Svir's sleeve.

"The Rebels have artillery, sir. I don't know how. They wiped out our main force in half a day. My own reconnaissance group followed the Rebels into Doomsday area. They met the Provincial Loyalists at Kotta-svo-Picchiu. The city was razed. We left then. Apparently they saw us. Overtook us in one of our own fastboats."

The admiral gasped, and Svir could imagine his surprise. *Artillery?* Reliable, accurate artillery? So the Crownesse military no longer had a monopoly on the ultimate weapon.

But the admiral was shocked by the wrong thing, thought Svir. Kotta-svo-Picchiu had housed the second-largest telescope in the world. The insolent inhabitants of the Doomsday Province often insisted that the Queen use the Kotta Eye for her projects, rather than the High Eye at the top of Heavensgate Mountain. Marget was not going to be happy about this turn of events.

CHAPTER 9

Svir wriggled, delighted in his dry uniform. It was amazing how good the feel of cloth sliding freely across skin could be. Thank goodness these ministerial conferences were held in a dryroom—at least the Bayfastlings wanted their maps and documents kept dry. The meeting room was deep within the Crown Keep. Along the walls of the room were racks of maps and overlays—one of Marget's innovations. Around the oval table sat the ten top ministers of Crownesse. All were dressed in plain black uniforms. Sometimes Svir thought these Bureaucrats were ostentatiously plain in their worship of the utilitarian. Only once in a generation did they wear their dress uniforms.

Tatja Grimm was standing at the narrow end of the table, a map pointer in her hand. As Queen of Crownesse she was expected to dress lavishly at all times—but at these cabinet meetings she could usually get away with a sequined semiskirt and silk blouse. Her long red hair was combed smoothly over her shoulders and draped with casual perfection across her blouse. It was hard to believe, but she was nearly thirty years old. The only clue to her age was the faint desperation that Svir sometimes saw in her look. He could see that desperation now. Probably he knew her better than anyone, and when she was really upset she often lost her ability to gauge the understanding of her audience; sometimes her speech became so terribly elliptical that only a mindreader could have any idea what she was talking about. Other times—as in the present case—she went to great lengths to explain the obvious.

At the moment she was discussing the large wall map that showed the coast of The Continent stretching west and northward from Bayfast. The four thousand-mile-long

Doomsday Mountain Range separated a three-hundred-mile-wide coastal strip from the interior of The Continent. That coastal strip was the greatest cereal-production area in the world and one of the Crown's most prized possessions. Now the northernmost province of that strip, Picchiu, had revolted against the authority of the Crown.

"Fortunately," Tatja was saying, "Sfierranyi, the province bordering Picchiu on the south, has remained loyal to our rule, and has raised a large army to oppose the Picchiul Insurrectionists. Ten days ago we sent two thousand well-trained troops to land north of the Picchiui—here." She tapped the pointer on a spot some ten miles south of Kotta-svo-Picchiu at the border of Doomsday Province. "Doomsday refused to supply troops," she grimaced, "but we had hoped to trap the Insurrectionists between our well-trained troops on the North, and the Sfierranyil horde on the south.

"Gentles, we were stomped. Our so-called shock troops were decimated. If it had not been for the 'undisciplined' Sfierranyii, the Insurrectionists would have made their independence good. Instead, the Loyalists chased the Rebels north, to the Picchiu River. In the most recent battle we have knowledge of, Kotta-svo-Picchiu was destroyed. We are now fighting a war on the very borders of Doomsday Province.

"In its own way, this is as bad for us as if the Picchiui had been victorious. The Doomsdaymen need small excuse to declare their independence of us. Their lands are beyond the effective range of our military forces. The destruction of Kotta-svo-Picchiu—a Doomsday city, despite its name—gives them excuse. The forty-inch reflecting telescope just outside the city was destroyed." She took a deep breath. "Gentles, you know I have my . . . quirks. One of them is a profound love for things astronomical. I needed that telescope. I also need the good will of the Doomsdaymen to give me access to their other large telescope—the High Eye. I want to retain control of the Doomsday area." She glared at the Bureaucrats, and Svir knew she saw the faint signs of amusement and relief on the ministers' faces. Doomsday Province was important to them for its metals production—not its astrological/astronomical cult. And they were relieved that her commands did not conflict with national interest. The Bureaucrats were loyal, but some monarchs had set the Nation back years with fanatical hobbies. It was nice to have a Queen with innocuous interests. Tatja smiled and turned to the Minister of Information. "All right, Wechsler, what do your spies say?"

Haarm Wechsler stood up and moved to the head of the table. Wechsler barely topped five feet, and weighed not more than ninety pounds. But as Minister of Information, he was a man with a long lever. He controlled the most extensive espionage operations in history. He bowed spastically to Tatja. "Thank you, Marget. In these last few hours I've reviewed the reports that Lieutenant Mörl brought from my agents Upcoast. The picture these reports mosaic is a strange one. As far as we have known till now, the Picchiul Assembly simply passed a resolution declaring that Your Majesty—your pardon—achieved power through fraud. This was so obviously ridiculous that we ignored it—until the Assembly further resolved to sever its connections with what it claimed was an unlawful government here in Bayfast. This is the superficial picture. But my agents report that these actions are due to the intrigues of one Oktar Profirio. Profirio is an elusive individual—and apparently a preternaturally talented one. He is a member of the Provincial Assembly—an appointee—replacing a member who died last year. That appointment was on, uh, the thirty-seventh of Summer, nine hundred and thirty-five. Before that date he had no fame whatsoever." Wechsler set his notes on the table and looked about the room impressively. "In fact, *I* suspect the name is an alias. Though Profirio sounds like an Upcoast name, there is no clan in Picchiu which bears it."

Tatja interrupted. "It could indeed be an alias, Minister Wechsler. But about thirty years ago a family of poor nobles named Profirchte moved from the Tsanart Islands to Picchiu. I understand that they changed their name to Profirio."

The Minister of Information flushed. It was well known that he had the ego of ten men, and a sarcastic wit to match. Rarely had he been put down—and by a superior he could not rebut except with fact. It was this occasional display of omniscience that more than anything else kept the top ministers of Crownesse personally loyal to Tatja Grimm.

"Uh, yes, Marget, I was not aware of that. However, and be that as it may," he rushed ahead, "Oktar Profirio is the individual responsible for the introduction of artillery into the Rebel arsenal. He produced the designs for accurate and stable barrels. And of course, Your Majesty is aware that, of all things, this is the development which makes artillery the deadly weapon it is. Our wooden gun-tubes are both stable and accurate, but it took nearly half a century to develop them. Apparently Profirio achieved the same in less than half a year. He is either a magician or a defector from our own military. Personally I have never believed in magicians." No one laughed. "Anyway, the troops we sent Upcoast were very lightly equipped —no art'ry, no cavalry, no weapons heavier than the standard crossbow. It is no surprise that they were smashed, now that we know of the enemy's advantage. Profirio's men may be provincial rabble, but his guns are damn accurate.

"What is a surprise, though, is that somehow the Loyalist Sfierranyil army also has artillery. The most recent reports are from my Picchiul agents. They aren't too specific about the Sfierranyii. Apparently the Loyalists managed to steal some of Profirio's guns. Without this theft, the perfidious Profirio would without doubt now control all Picchiu Province. As it turned out, the Loyalists chased him north into Kotta-svo-Picchiu. The Rebel command took refuge in rooms beneath the observatory there. Loyalist fire destroyed that complex, and much of the city. We know Profirio escaped with a large part of his army—"

"Excuse me, Minister Wechsler," said Svir.

"Certainly. Don't hesitate to ask your question, my man."

Svir ignored Wechsler's patronizing tone. "About the men who report from some vantage point on the accuracy of the artillery fire—"

"You're thinking of the Forward Art'ry Observators."

"Yes, that's who I mean. With all this rain, how can they report back to the artillery batteries with fire control directions? I mean, isn't there some new communication technique involved here?"

Wechsler stared for a moment. Obviously the question hadn't occurred to him. Without FAO's, artillery was blind, and therefore, practically useless. Then he saw the answer and smiled. "You've been studying the stars so long, I fear, that you have forgotten the state of things here on the ground. The farther north you go, the more the climate becomes a mixture of arctic and monsoonal. At the fortieth parallel, the latitude of Kotta-svo-Picchiu, there are a number of clear days, even during the Waterfall. So heliographs may be used efficiently and—"

"Besides," spoke Tatja as she stood up, "we're talking about the foothills of the Doomsday range. This is rugged country. If the Sfierranyil art'ry were based on the highlands south of the river, the gunmen would be in the line of sight of Kotta-svo-Picchiu—so they would not need Forward Observators." She walked swiftly to the head of the table and motioned Haarm Wechsler to be seated. Her comment had an absent-minded tone.

Usually Tatja let these cabinet meetings drag on and on till the ministers actually thought that the plans decided upon were their own. But Svir had noticed that whenever she was sincerely upset, she would let everybody talk for a while, then break in and tell the ministers—in great detail—how to do their jobs. This was exactly what she did now. "I think we all have the facts now. The rest of you have seen the other reports that the fastboat brought back. Through no fault of your own, we've been smashed. Because of the art'ry, both Loyalists and Rebels have suffered many casualties. According to the reports, Profirio still has thirteen thousand five hundred men and two hundred gun tubes of six-inch caliber. Apparently the Sfierranyii have something like eight thousand five hundred men and perhaps one hundred and fifty gun tubes. North of Profirio are the uncommitted Doomsdaymen.

"We've three goals: to prevent the destruction of any more astronomical artifacts, to destroy Profirio's army, and to capture Oktar Profirio himself." There was an uneasy shifting about at these goals. The high ministers saw no particular necessity for the first and third.

"Now, here is how we will accomplish these goals." She

sat down and spoke more rapidly and with less inflection. "In four or five days the Waterfall will end, and we will be in the Turnabout. Before that happens we will dispatch every fastboat in our command Upcoast. I will accompany the expedition." About the table, Svir saw the incredulous faces—the Crown never went on military expeditions. "We won't bother with ships of the line. They're too slow and would be caught in the Turnabout when their progress would be even slower. I figure we can transport something like fifteen thousand men with supporting equipment and art'ry by fastboat alone. This time we won't make the mistake of trying a pincers movement in coordination with the Loyalists. We'll land on the Loyalist side of the lines and take advantage of the mountains and the Doomsdaymen to keep the enemy from retreating further north.

"Here is the order of operations: the Three hundred and thirty-sixth and Four hundred and third Infantry Battle Groups will compose the landing force, with the direct support of the Twenty-fifth and Fiftieth Art'ry Batteries. At present the following fastboats are in Bayfast harbor: Five to Eight, Eleven, Thirteen, Seventeen to Thirty-five . . ." The high ministers recovered from their shock and began writing as fast as they were able. (Stenographers were barred from cabinet meetings.) Once before, Marget had rattled off a battle plan like this. The awful thing was that no matter how off-the-cuff her comments seemed, they hung together when they were checked with the facts. Marget apparently knew her military establishment to a depth greater than any career military man. Her orders extended down to the third level of organization. It would have taken the military staffs of the various services ten days of coordinated planning to produce the order she was creating now.

The first time this happened there had been audible snickers from the ministers. They had repeatedly stopped and questioned her. That had been the only time Svir could remember when Tatja had shown rage. It had certainly equaled the intensity attributed to the Mad Kings of the sixth and seventh centuries. Several ministers had reverted to common status after that incident. Experience is a good teacher—and Tatja's plans always turned out to be brilliant—so this time no one interrupted with questions or suggestions. It was probably the most efficient and one-sided committee meeting in history. Tatja spoke for nearly half an hour.

Finally she stopped. The ministers looked at their notes and saw with glazed relief that the order was complete. She smiled pleasantly and asked, "Are there any questions?" There was an exhausted chorus of "No" from around the table. It would be several hours before they or their aides could devise any questions. "Very well," said Tatja, "I will be available to answer any questions that do occur to you. If there is to be any deviation from the plan, I want to hear of it immediately. Remember, I don't believe in delegating decisions. It's another of my—quirks. I expect to be on my way by the night wake period tomorrow. I'll see you then, if not earlier."

It was a dismissal. Svir followed the others as they started for the door. He didn't know whether to be relieved or disappointed. The plan did not require his services. He had rather enjoyed watching the other ministers sweat a little—especially Wechsler. On the other hand, this bolstered his suspicions that his post was a sop for his silence. With a great show of courtesy he offered Haarm Wechsler the door. Wechsler grunted and walked out. Just then Tatja spoke. "Stay a minute, Svir." From the corner of his eye, Svir saw Wechsler's retreating back stiffen at these words. He could imagine the other's suspicions and puzzlement.

When the others had left and the door had been shut, Tatja spoke again. "Have a seat, Svir. I didn't include you in my order of operations because your duties will depend on factors I can't predict, while the military situation will probably work according to plan—though not the plan I just gave our friends." Svir sat back in the chair, rather enjoying being the confidant of the most powerful person in the world. "I have a feeling that we are going to be dealing with the Doomsdaymen. Ostensibly we needed their support in order to keep this Profirio from retreating further north. As an astronomer, you are really the only cabinet member who can speak to their priests with some sympathy. And I know they respect your work in astronometry."

"But you would be just as competent to handle them."

"Sure, and I'm competent to do anything my cabinet ministers can do. But there's only one of me. I want you to bring along Ancho, too."

Svir hesitated. His next question would probably provoke a lecture on the strained supply situation. But then he could use the argument that Cor was now more adept with Ancho than himself.

"Could my wife come along?" he asked, and braced himself.

"Certainly. Don't you see, Svir? During this operation, there will be times when my actions are so contrary to the interests of Crownesse that the ministers will balk. Since the Mad Kings, the civil service has found ways of defending itself against the arbitrary ruler—and still maintain a tradition of selfless loyalty to the Crown. I need some people with me who are outside the civil service structure—people I can trust. There are really only three people I trust. You and Cor are two of them. You know enough about my motives to go along with my plans even when they seem absurd to my faithful ministers."

Her frankness was a welcome change from the usual intrigue and deception she used to get what she wanted. It was a comfortable feeling to be on the inside of a conspiracy for once.

She sat back in her chair. Svir had seen this change before, but it always seemed spectacular to him. At one moment she was taut, intense, directing an intermesh of plans that stretched across the planet and beyond. Then, in an instant, she was a relaxed, seductive woman.

"I only wish Ked Maccioso were here too. He has most of your qualifications—and he's a native of Picchiu. By now he's probably over his indignation about the way I handled him and the Barge. If only this had happened when the Tarulle people weren't on the other side of the world."

She languidly crossed her long, smooth legs. Her right hand seemed to derive its own private sybaritic pleasure as it moved over the smooth fabric of her skirt. Her eyes were half closed, her lips barely parted in a dreamy smile. Svir felt sudden guilt. In this moment he felt the same intense attraction for her that she had originally used to hook him into her plans. He wanted so much to go to her, put his arms around her—all the more so because now he was sure that she wasn't pretending, that in fact she had forgotten his presence. He hunted desperately for something to break this chain of thought.

Then he guessed the cause of her sudden mood. "You really think Wechsler's 'Perfidious Profirio' is a godling in disguise?"

"Mmm," the satisfied sound came from deep in her throat. "There's a good chance. It's that time of the century, you know. He could be a defector from our own art'ry craftsmen, but I think Haarm Wechsler's spies would have discovered that if it were the case. If he's not a defector, then he's probably of my—caliber. There is no straightforward solution to the problem of making practical artillery pieces from nonmetallics. A rather complete grasp of ceramic and impregnation chemistry is required. Even then, several years of trial and error experimentation are needed unless you use maximation techniques that I've never bothered to write up. And if Profirio had more than two hundred tubes constructed in just two quarters, then he's using standardized production methods that I've never seen before. If only he is what he seems to be." A frown crossed her face at this point, and her business personality nearly surfaced. Then the frown disappeared, as she twisted comfortably in her chair.

Svir got up and moved toward the door. The fact that her desire was not directed at him had no effect on his desire for her. He vaguely wondered what violence would greet an advance on his part. And this thought made him feel even more guilty. If he left now perhaps he could forget the feeling.

Just as he reached the door, he remembered the narrow folder he was carrying. Damn. His escape must be delayed a few moments. He returned and set the folder on the table before Tatja. "Marget"—he used the official name-of-address—"here are the latest reports from the High Eye."

Her eyes came open wide, and her back straightened with a little start. She didn't seem irritated at the interruption, just a little dazed, almost bewildered, as if she had been awakened from deep sleep. "Uh, oh yes. Thanks."

He turned to go. "Stick around, Svir. I just want to page

through these, and you can have them back." She read the compact, complex reports faster than he could browse light fiction. Finally she came to the last sheet of stiff white parchment. Svir remembered this report was one of the most peculiar he had seen in a long time. He wondered what her reaction would be. He looked over her shoulder at the sheet. There were the typical salutations which, in the case of the Doomsday astronomers, he was sure were meant to be insulting. The Doomsdaymen had always resented the authority of Crownesse, submitting only because that power was comparatively innocuous and could protect them from nearer enemies. They hadn't counted on the rise of Tatja Grimm, who exercised an unwelcome interest in all things astronomical, and who required quarterly reports of astronomical activity from the Doomsday observatory. At first they had patronizingly referred her to the standard journals where a few of their results appeared. Even now that they sent her a complete report, Svir felt they did it with an air of condescension. The report began:

Spring 12, 936 YD

To Her Most Gracious Majesty, Marget of Sandros, Queen of All Crownesse, High Mayor of Bayfast, Lady Protector of the Coasts and Deserts, Greeting: Herein we present the 769th consecutive astronomical report of our humble search across the Face of God. We beg Your Majesty's indulgence with this unworthy and trivial tabulation entitled:

"Six Abnormal Objects in the Constellation of the Running Thief"

In the course of a routine sky patrol session, picture plate number 2879 was exposed at approximately 2:30 Picchiu Meridian Time on the 9th of Summer, 935. A new object of magnitude 10 was revealed by this exposure. Ten acolytes were assigned the task of maintaining a night-round watch on this area of the sky with the 12" reflector at the observatory.

(Svir winced at this offhand reference to what must have been one of the most tortuous projects in the history of astronomy. He could scarcely bear to imagine sitting in the cold and rarefied air, twenty hours a night—watching for a barely visible twinkle light-years away. The Doomsday astronomers were famed for this sort of sadomasochism.)

During the next ninety days, the images of five more such objects were captured on picture plates. Data concerning all six objects are tabulated below.

Obj Nr	Began (PMT)	Date	RA*	Dec	Max Mag	Duration (Minutes)
1	c2:30	Summer 9, 935	90°32'19".4	23°14'25".1	10.1**	?(200)
2	1:07:56	Summer 27, 935	90°31'56".9	23°14'25".1	11.6	35
3	40:00:39	Summer 45, 935	90°31'46".8	23°14'25".1	12.5	31
4	38:56:17	Autumn 17, 935	90°31'41".8	23°14'25".1	13.1	31
5	37:54:13	Autumn 35, 935	90°31'40".3	23°14'25".1	13.6	30
6	36:53:04	Winter 8, 936	90°31'41".4	23°14'25".1	14.0	29

*According to our amended usage, O°RA is the zenith meridian at the High Eye on the 1st of Winter, 920 YD, at 40:00:00 PMT. Right ascension increases in the same sense as the sun travels across the Celestial Face.
**The magnitude given for (1) depends on the assumption that the object was uniformly bright during the plate's exposure, which is a reasonable approximation if the light curve of (1) were similar to the other objects.

Objects (2) through (6) were subjected to spectrographic examination. Their light appears entirely due to continuum radiation. The light curves for objects (2) through (6) appear identical except for the overall change in magnitude, indicated above by the column for maximum magnitude achieved.

The 90/23 region was below our horizon at the critical time of evening of the 26th of Winter. However, a close watch of this area will be maintained in the coming quarters.

This concludes the 769th report of astronomical activities to Your Majesty. It was prepared by Your Majesty's unworthy servant R. Kels, Archobserver and Chief Instrumentalist to the High Eye.

Tatja stared at the report for a full ten seconds. When it came, her laughter was explosive. She doubled up in her chair and her face became red. Finally she sat up and wiped tears from her eyes. "Talk about 'words writ large upon the sky,' " she gasped.

Svir picked up the report and looked at it once more. He could guess what she meant by that remark, but he couldn't see how the lights described could be a message. It certainly was an abnormal sequence, but did she think that every unexplained phenomenon was evidence of extraplanetary intelligence?

She saw his look. "You mean you don't see it?"

He put on pedant's armor and answered evasively. "With only the information presented in this report, I don't. Perhaps you're making your conclusions on something not in the report, on information I don't have."

"Oh, I suppose that's possible," she said slowly. "But you *are* an astronomer. At least that's what you keep telling me. But perhaps you aren't aware of the key facts necessary to solve this puzzle: there are four quarters to a year, forty-five days to a quarter, forty hours to a day, sixty minutes to an hour, and sixty seconds to a minute. Light travels at one hundred and eighty-six thousand miles per second, and what's more"—she pretended to strain after some subtle detail—"oh yes, the world revolves about the sun at a distance of eighty-five million miles, and not vice versa—as you may have been led to believe. Got all that?"

"Urk." Svir felt his face become hot, and wondered what obvious point he had missed in his analysis of the report. "I'll give it another look," he said, backing toward the door.

CHAPTER 10

Svir had always harbored a deep dislike for skoats. Since they were rare on the Chainpearl Islands, he had seen only one or two before he came to The Continent, where they were the most common draft and riding animal. He felt uneasy just riding in a vehicle drawn by the fat brown quadrupeds, and now he was actually riding one! He glanced warily at the long brown neck and pointed ears in front of him. He was yet to be convinced of his skoat's gentle disposition. The animal had the unsettling habit of bringing its neck around and taking a so-called playful nip at his camouflage uniform. And even if the beast turned out to be as gentle as Cor claimed it was, this was still the most uncomfortable ride he had ever been treated to. His rear felt like one vast bruise, and his legs ached fiercely from being splayed over the tubby animal's back. What's more, the skoat *smelled,* and the acrid sweat from its short fur mixed itchily with his own perspiration.

He lurched forward as the skoat shifted balance going down a steep hill. The road the army followed was nearly ten feet wide—and paved. It was probably the second-best overland road in this part of The Continent. But they were already well into the coastal highlands south of the Picchiu River, and the road went up and down almost as many miles as it went across. Svir's battle group headed into a narrow valley. Almost two hundred feet below, he could see the narrow stream that over the millenia had gouged this channel through the limestone. As they descended, the sunlight was filtered through progressively thicker layers of leaves until they were surrounded by a bright green twilight. It was cool and pleasant. The air moved slowly and was laden with the musty smell of hundreds of years of decomposing leaves. This scent was strange to Svir, since he had never seen a deciduous tree before.

The tranquility of the scene barely penetrated his more immediate discomforts.

He urged his mount across the clear, swift-moving stream at the bottom of the valley, then twisted about in his saddle and looked back. Where was everyone? Only the gun carriage immediately behind him was visible. Through the trees he could hear the creaking of hundreds of carriage wheels and the snorts and clatter of a thousand skoats, but he couldn't see a one. As his own mount climbed the north side of the little valley, he finally saw them. When they moved through dense greenery, the camouflage splotch paint rendered the army virtually invisible. The effect was frightening. The only visual cues to all this activity were the outlines of the vehicles and animals as they moved down the south side of the valley—those outlines as faint and yet definite as the refraction patterns of super-heated air rising from a fire.

Then there was a louder clatter, and Svir saw a rider overtaking him. He slowed down and saw that it was his wife. Coronadas Ascuasenya urged her animal up the slope with baby talk and lots of enthusiasm. He couldn't get over the fact that she was actually fond of the creatures—and even thought she could talk to them. He put her superior riding ability to the fact that she had grown up on the Llerenitos where skoats were popular.

"Hi, Cor," he said. He reached over, but could barely touch her shoulder. Kissing a girl on skoatback is virtually impossible.

Cor held his hand for a moment. Svir continued, "I thought you were supposed to stay in Marget's carriage with Ancho." Cor had been under strict orders to remain in the carriage, but he felt happy she had chosen to mutiny.

She retorted, "No, she tells me to stay with Ancho, period. And if you can't see that's what I'm doing, then perhaps I'll take up some other male." Svir looked more closely and saw that there was a bulge under her blouse where no bulge should be. A second later a pair of pointed ears and brown eyes pushed out of that bulge and looked seriously at him.

"Besides," said Cor, "we got four hours of sleep, and wanted to be with you."

"Uk," Svir felt a certain amount of jealousy at this. The expedition from Crownesse had landed her in Picchiu Province just after sunrise—nearly twenty-five hours ago. It had taken almost five hours to get equipment, troops, and skoats off the fastboats. They—rather Tatja and her generals—had decided to ride straight through the afternoon without sleep: in three longitudes there was no Seraph to twilight the night. The sun was still at least five hours above the horizon. Svir wondered whether he could hold out till dark. He was actually falling asleep in his saddle, a feat he would have sworn to be impossible just fifteen hours before. How the infantrymen kept going he couldn't guess.

But the strategy was sound. The expeditionary force was nearing the battle zone. Soon they would actually enter the Loyalist camp and incidentally come under Rebel art'ry fire. How exciting.

They were moving up a long, gentle slope. The crest was about four hundred yards away. The tree cover was light, but there was still much shade. He looked through the trees to his left, toward the east. The foothills of the Doomsday Range lay brown and green and gray. Beyond them, so far away and yet so clearly etched white against the sky, stood the highest peaks of the range. On He'gate, the highest peak, was the Doomsday observatory. The view brought him wide awake.

"Svir, look up front." He squinted at the riders clumped together up ahead. He thought he recognized Tatja and the colonel in charge of point security. At least it was the colonel's skoat. But what was that officer doing this far back in the column? Evidently they were talking to someone standing on the ground. The colonel moved aside, and Svir saw that his guess had been correct. The dismounted fellow was suited in maroon, and he wore a strangely plumed hat. Had they finally reached the outskirts of the Loyalists' concentration?

The colonel wheeled about and waved to the troops. The command was immediately translated by the sergeant driving the nearest team of art'ry skoats. "Hard hats!" the little sergeant shouted as she donned her own. Svir reluctantly reached for his own reinforced-web-plastic helmet, set it on his head, and fastened the chin strap. He had once thought the head armor looked rather dashing, but now he discovered that the inside of the helmet was infernally hot.

Around him the column was changing into an extended rank, about fifty yards from the crest of the hill. It took more than two hours to bring up the rear of the train. He watched with some wonder as the infantrymen double-timed into position.

Finally the fifteen thousand troopers were assembled. There was a pause. For two miles in either direction the irregular line of skoats, guns, and men stood waiting to plunge forward into the field of enemy observation.

A clear-toned whistle sounded. The army surged over the crest and started down the other side. Ahead of them the road descended gently, then rose toward the crest of a second ridge some two or three miles away. And miles beyond the second, he could make out yet another ridge. The greenery extended peacefully about four hundred yards to their front. But beyond that the landscape was interrupted by deep craters and circular patches of burned grass. The near side of the hill they were approaching was covered with wide black splotches. Vast areas of burned-out trees were like monstrous black mold. The usually pleasant smell of charred wood came strongly across the valley. Svir looked at his wife. She was gently talking her skoat forward. Ancho had disappeared inside her blouse.

The army descended rapidly, and Svir found himself praying that somehow they could escape enemy observation and gain the blackened hill ahead. Soon they would be so far into the valley that they would be invisible to enemy observers beyond their objective.

Then the sky exploded. Two hundred yards to the front, a line of orange-red fireballs hung forty feet in the air. A second later Svir's head was snapped back and his helmet clanged. He reached up automatically and felt a quarter-inch shrapnel bullet imbedded in his helmet. He watched glassy-eyed as the fireballs became innocent black puffs of smoke and blew away. What would it be like when the enemy got the range and timing better? Only the general movement of the troops kept him going forward.

The army broke into squares, one battle group forward, the next back, so as to avoid complete catastrophe if the curtain of fire ever came on target. But the enemy was about twelve miles away, and the corrected fire was thirty seconds coming: the nearest burst was high explosive, time-fused, and it made the shrapnel sound like a popped paper bag. He felt the blow through his whole body. His skoat staggered to its knees, and he was tossed backwards, out of the saddle. He grabbed at air, his mind filled with visions of landing on the ground and being trampled. Then his mount surged back to its feet and he found himself seated safely yet awkwardly on the rear of the animal, behind the saddle. He scrambled into the saddle as the animal galloped forward.

Cor! He looked wildly about and saw her coming up from behind him through the smoke. Her lower face was covered with blood. She came abreast of him and shouted, "You hurt bad?"

"That's what I was going to ask you," he gasped back. He noticed that his jaw was bloody, too. They both had nosebleeds. "Come on." They were already falling behind their battle group. They swerved about a large area of burning grass and regained their positions.

The formation finally reached the bottom of the valley—now they were hidden from enemy observation. Enemy accuracy lessened as the formation began evasive maneuvers. The air became clearer, and Svir no longer choked on dust and smoke.

Casualties had apparently been light during the fifteen-minute encounter. The horsemen's nylon armor had protected them from most of the shrapnel. At their far right flank an impact-fused HE shell went off next to an art'ry piece. Svir watched in amazement as the gun tube was thrown spinning high into the air.

His ears buzzed from the punishment they had received, and all other sounds were muffled. The land was black except for flickering yellow halos of flame around three skeletons. The blue sky above the haze seemed blasphemous next to this hellish landscape. They were eighty yards from the crest now. Shells still burst, but the enemy's aim, at least for Svir's battle group, was wildly inaccurate. Of the other battle groups, he could not be so sure. The ridge line was marked with numerous defiles which made observation difficult. He could see no more than half of the fifteen thousand men of his own battle group. The formation's forward movement ceased. Supply vehicles moved to the guns they were to feed. The rear elements of the battle group spread out to parallel the ridge line. The air was filled with the sounds of whining skoats, creaking wagons, shouting men. These last were not confused sounds, but the efficient direction of officers who knew exactly what they wanted and were working with well-trained troops.

The group was preparing for art'ry battle. A gun carriage pulled up even with Svir and Cor. The driver leaped to the ground and raced to the front of her skoats. She unfastened their harnesses and led them away from the art'ry piece. The gunmen on top of the carriage moved just as efficiently. They were performing a much-practiced task, and there was no talk or wasted motion. Two of the gunmen unlashed the weapon as the other two passed a six-inch shell up from the supply wagon. Around them ran infantrymen, their crossbows at port arms. Svir couldn't imagine how they could run after the long day's march, but the troopers were really moving. The soldiers disappeared into the smoke as they ran toward the crest to set up front security. Evidently that smoke was not due to enemy action—it kept getting thicker, and Svir could hear grenades popping in the distance. He looked back at the gunmen. The piece was loaded now and the heavy plastic breach closed. A courier from the FAOs read fire control directions to the gunmen. The greenish barrel was cranked up. The enemy would get a surprising reply to his own attack. Through the haze, Svir could see other gun carriages, hear their breeches being slammed shut. Then came a pause. Fire instructions were received. Weapons were aimed and loaded. He could imagine this scene in every one of the ten battle groups, stretched up and down the ridge line. The preparations were complete, and now the war machine waited for the command that would set it in motion.

Three minutes passed, and still no action. Through the buzzing in his ears, he heard Cor say something. He turned to her. "What's that?"

Her voice seemed muffled, "I asked, where are the Sfierranyil Loyalists?"

He started. Cor's question was a good one. Everyone around them wore the camouflage suits of the Crown's Men. The only provincial he had seen that afternoon had been the fellow talking to Tatja and the point colonel. He looked about quickly, half expecting to see enemy bowmen spring from spider holes. This unpleasant line of thought was broken a moment later as he saw an officer riding down the firing line, shouting an indistinct command.

The gunmen looked up in momentary surprise, then began unloading their weapons. As they did so, the forward infantrymen came back across the hill. Svir gaped. The situation reminded him of stories he had heard about unit commands given to recruits during training. The people at the top apparently could not make up their minds. Either Tatja had been hit on the head or she was being devious.

The troops and art'ry reformed and resumed their march—though now they were moving east, parallel to the crest of the hill. Svir sighed and urged his animal forward. It was at least an hour till sunset, and at this latitude twilight would last three hours.

He sidled toward the nearest gun carriage and called to the driver. "What's the story?" The girl looked at him—his camouflage bore no rank insignia. Her answer was an obscenity, roughly equivalent to "We were shafted."

He fell back a bit and walked beside the art'ry carriage. The gunman sitting there was more talkative. "That's right. We got it up to here." He motioned. "There's only one decent reason for racing over that hill in daylight—and that's to get our pieces in range and let the other side have a taste of their own poison. If we weren't going to engage the enemy, we should've stayed back there"—he waved at the hill to the south—"until dark, and then come across. Instead we lost men—*for nothing*!" For a moment the gunman seemed to wonder if he might be talking to someone in authority, but he was too mad to care. "Somebody made a damn stupid mistake." Svir found himself nodding. The situation was even more fouled up than he had thought. Perhaps Tatja had been killed as they moved across the valley—and the subsequent change in plan had been the result of some incompetent's vacillation. But no Crownesse general officer could be so incompetent. That left provincial treachery as the most likely cause of the present situation.

Behind them the sun moved slowly toward the horizon and sent rose and orange glows across the sky. In the far distance stood the high peaks of the Doomsday range, the world's ragged edge. They left the cratered, burning land behind, and soon there was only the smell of grass and living trees. If he hadn't been in the saddle for the last twenty hours, he might have enjoyed the scene. He slumped forward, trying to find some way to keep his balance in spite of the dizzy sleepiness that flowed over him in progressively more overpowering waves. Cor rode beside him, and he was thankful she didn't try to make cheerful conversation.

He didn't notice the sun set, but eventually he saw that the sky was dark, and the ground gray. Ahead the Doomsday peaks were still in the sun's light. They formed a jagged red band hanging in limbo above the darkened, nearer lands.

Then someone was pushing at his shoulder, calling to him. He sat erect and looked about. It was nearly dark. The sky was clear, but there were only stars in it—Seraph's familiar light was missing. "We're here," Cor said.

At first glance the forest around them seemed uninhabited, but then he saw the tents hidden at irregular intervals in the brush. Further away he could hear the *grunchunch* of browsing skoats. The Crown's Men had finally reached the Sfierranyil Loyalists. Svir slipped from his saddle and leaned against the skoat. A shadow approached.

"Svo keechoritte bignioru?" it asked.

Svir was about to croak, *"Sagneori Sfierro"* (I don't speak Sfierro) when Cor cut in with, *"Attrupa bignoro chispuer, sfiorgo malmu."* He remembered with relief that Sfierro was quite closely related to Cor's native Llereno.

"Traeche ke," the other said and led them some two hundred feet into the brush. As far as Svir could tell there

were no tents nearby. Finally the Sfierranyi stopped, pointed to a flat brushless area, and gabbled something more. "He says we can put up our tent here," Cor said. Svir felt like crying. He doubted if he had enough coordination left even to unpack the tent from the skoat's back. The Sfierranyi solved that problem by unhitching the tent pack and dropping it to the ground. Then he grabbed the skoats' reins and led them away to the tethering area.

Svir looked stupidly at the barely visible gray patch that was the folded tent. Itchybites buzzed about in the moist, cool air. The tiny bastards would feed well tonight. He fell to his knees and tried to unfasten the tent buckles. Cor joined him. Soon they had the tent spread flat on the ground. He slipped the center pole through the hole in the top layer of tent fabric and fastened it. Cor crawled inside and spread the floor rods.

Then they were both inside. The ground seemed so soft. He reached for Cor, and she came easily into his arms. His kiss became a snore and he was asleep.

Cor grinned in the darkness. "This is no good, friend. Tomorrow, you get some sleep during the day."

CHAPTER 11

"Listen, you pack of traitors. You cost us thirty-five men and three art'ry pieces this afternoon. We're going to have an explanation or we're going to have your heads!" In the flickering torchlight, Haarm Wechsler's face appeared even paler than usual. "For the last two hours you've led us a merry chase all over this camp. But now we've found you." He stopped and stood a little taller. The Crownesse Guardsmen behind him came to attention. "Now you can answer for your infidelity to Marget herself."

Everyone in the room—Provincial and Bayfastling—came to his feet. Tatja entered the Sfierranyil command tent and looked about. Close behind her came three general officers. Her lips parted in a faint smile and she murmured to Wechsler, "Spare us the fireworks, will you, Haarm?" She advanced to the table at the center of the room and sat down. "Won't you be seated, my gentles." Behind her the Crownesse people uneasily took their seats. They believed they were among enemies. On the other side of the table, the Sfierranyil commanders seemed equally upset. Most of the provincial commanders were old men. Though they weren't the best campaigners in the world, they should at least have been loyal. She recognized most of them from the dossiers Wechsler kept. Only the man immediately opposite her was unfamiliar.

Her tone was pleasant as she began. "Now that we are all here, I would like some answers. You deceived us this afternoon. Your courier told us you needed immediate artillery support. When we came to your aid, we found you were moving away from us. This misunderstanding cost us men and equipment, and I ask for some explanation." Her reasonable tone took some of the edge off Wechsler's previous statement of the question.

A high-ranking militiaman stood and bowed deeply, his chest of medals glittering faintly. He wiped his hand back through his hair, leaving the white tangle even more disordered than before. The Sfierranyil officer had the air of a man disgraced. Even his epaulets drooped. Surprisingly his Spräk was without accent. "Marget, what you say is true. There was deception. We can only beg your mercy. We deceived you because we were deceived ourselves. We, uh, our training is not as thorough as might be desired by Your Majesty. We were required in defense of Your Crown to operate far outside our own province. To the north is our enemy and the Doomsdaymen—which latter refuse us aid. To the south is Picchiu Province—whose army is our enemy." The old man paused. His rambling had taken him so far afield that he didn't remember his point. Tatja grabbed Wechsler by the elbow as that worthy prepared to make some cutting comments about Sfierranyil mental acuteness. After all, she found normal people almost as redundant as this one. Then the militiaman had regained the thread of his talk. "Marget, the course of our campaign has taken us further and yet further inland, as we followed the forces of the Rebel Profirio. We never guessed that your aid would come to us from the south—for even in your omnipotence we didn't believe you could know we were this far from the coast. So we mistook you for Picchiul reinforcements pretending to be Crownesse troops. Thank God that you were so numerous that we could not attack you but only trick you into coming under Rebel fire. That's why we deceived you. And that's why, even when you arrived at this camp, we were circumspect in admitting you to our command area." The fellow's head bobbed up and down as he hunted for some hint of forgiveness in the Queen's face. Behind Tatja there was some easing of tension: the explanation was credible.

Tatja nodded. "Where is Profirio's main force now?"

"Uh, we believe that it's across the river and five miles upstream from here."

She raised an eyebrow. "How is that possible? This afternoon we were attacked by his artillery—and that was almost fifteen miles downstream from here." She produced a small piece of parchment and wrote rapidly upon it.

The young provincial sitting opposite Tatja touched the militiaman's sleeve and said, "*Dechemau,* Sam." The old man nodded and sat down gratefully.

As the young man stood, Tatja handed the parchment to a messenger and whispered something to him. The courier nodded and left. She turned back to the provincial staff. The young fellow was dark skinned, with straight black hair cut in the long Picchiul fashion. The expression on his narrow face was unworried—nearly sardonic. He wore the uniform of a full general in the provincial militia, but his chest bore not a single medal—which was unusual, since the Sfierranyil Militia gave medals for having fingernails clean.

"And who are you?" came Wechsler's irritating voice.

"Marget, I am Jolle. Until present difficulties I was a commercial chemist, but war makes different things of people, and the Provincial Assembly and the general staff elected me military commander of this expedition." There was a faint snort of disgust from the Crown's Men. They had a saying in the civil service that a nation which elects its generals elects defeat.

Jolle spoke rapidly. He had the right words but his Sfierro accent rendered them nearly unintelligible. "You see, Profirio has his art'ry split away from his infantry. So, in fact, I believe our misunderstanding this afternoon may give us a decisive advantage over the Rebels."

"Hmm, that would take some explaining."

Jolle nodded. "It's clear since the battle of Kotta-svo-Picchiu that Profirio is intensely interested in moving eastwards into the mountains. Of our several theories the most credible is that by moving into the heart of Doomsday territory he intends to somehow persuade the Doomsdaymen to join his insurrection. It's now apparent that this Profirio fellow has decided to gamble, to leave his art'ry behind and gain him greater speed. Since both our armies were in march, there was small chance we would exchange gunfire till we were well into the mountains. By that time he would be well ahead of us. In fact, I suspect he intended to interpose his troops between us and O'rmouth, Doomsday's capital, so *our* artillery fire would provoke the Doomsdaymen to enter the contest on his side, while at the same time, his own art'ry could follow both armies along the Riverside Road, which is a wide, level road and would provide them with swift transport. Thus he would end up with his art'ry on our flank and the Doomsday people against us, too.

"Unfortunately for him, his scheme hinged on the hope we would not discover his art'ry had been left behind, and this is the reason our misunderstanding is for the good. The commander Profirio left with the art'ry was by the appearance of your forces flustered—he opened fire, and destroyed his master's plan. Now, we know that his art'ry is hopelessly far behind, *we* can use the Riverside Road with impunity; we will thus get inland faster, and we will be in just the position he wanted to reserve for himself."

Tatja considered. The scheme described had ingenuity and daring of the caliber she sought. It was a deception that had failed only because of a subordinate's mistake and the unexpected appearance of her troops. There were still edges and ends that didn't fit, but the more she saw of this situation, the more she was convinced her goal was near.

How quiet everything was. It was late, and the animals of these lands had no Seraph to light their nights. The only sounds were insects creaking. It was hard to believe they were sitting in the midst of an armed camp. Inside the tent, things were quiet too. Even the officers who made some pretense of being awake sat with their eyes faintly glazed. A sound suspiciously like a snore came from behind her. These poor weak people—given thirty hours of hard work, they were dead on their feet.

She looked up and found Jolle's dark eyes gazing back. There was something unnatural about this one's accent. When she spoke, her question was not directly related to the events of that day. "Have you any idea where the Rebels got all this art'ry in the first place?"

Jolle shrugged. "Sorry. He raided the ammunition stockpiles Your Majesty keeps in the provinces. I've heard the fellow is a foreigner."

"Yes, I've, uh, suspected that. But where did you Loyalists get your artillery, Jolle?"

"Well, the ammunition as Profirio did."

"And the gun tubes?"

Jolle spread his hands in self-deprecation. "I am a chemist. I beg forgiveness if it displeases the Crown. I designed most of the artillery innovations you see among the Sfierranyii, but without them we would have had no chance to protect Your Majesty's interests from the Insurrectionists."

In that instant the silence seemed complete. One dark face filled the sensory universe and time itself slowed as she considered first one fantastic possibility and then another. The spell was broken as the door guard called a challenge to someone outside.

Svir came to abruptly, with the lightheaded alertness that follows a short, uneasy sleep. He swallowed painfully, trying to remove a nauseous taste from his mouth. "What do you want?" he croaked at the figure silhouetted in the entrance to the tent.

The shadowed shape whispered, "Sir, I have a message for you." The courier reached forward, and they fumbled in the darkness till Svir felt the parchment in his hand. He hunted about in his pack and came up with his matches. The flickering light was almost painfully bright. Cor came half-awake and mumbled something.

The courier blew the flame out. "We're under light security, sir. You can't do that," he said.

Svir's voice was as close to a scream as a whisper can be. "How in hell am I supposed to read this without a light!"

"I didn't make the rules, you—"

Svir was speechless for a second. Then he remembered that he was the person in authority and pulled rank. The messenger backed out of the tent, cowed. Svir carefully unsealed the flap, then lit another match, shielding it with his hand. The message was cryptically simple: "Azimuth 30°. Do it now—T." As he blew out the light, Cor rose on her elbows and asked, "What is it?"

"Tatja wants us to go ahead with the Plan. She says the azimuth is thirty degrees." He stuffed the message into his pocket and began gathering together the tripod and signaling equipment. Meanwhile Cor woke Ancho and fed him. The dorfox was not lively, and Svir knew they could expect trouble with him. Finally Cor convinced the little animal that there was a job to do. Ancho clung to her neck as she crawled out of the tent. Svir followed, dragging tripod and signaler.

For the moment it seemed to him that every sensation was intensified. He recognized the illusion. His balance was poor and he still had the most awful taste in his mouth. But this was actually the middle of the night wake period, as practiced in Bayfast. In fact, it was nearly lunchtime. The long daylight march and the different sleeping customs of the Upcoast people had inverted his normal schedule. He felt alert only because his natural time sense told him he should be.

The trees were close set. Insect sounds were loud and there were no signs of human activity. Svir peered up through the branches at the gray, faint light of the sky. There wasn't enough sky visible to recognize constellations. He and Cor moved cautiously along the indistinct path. The air was cool, but his uniform was still damp with sweat. He couldn't remember having felt more dirty or chilled.

He guided Cor northward. They moved up a slight slope. A man-shaped blotch could be seen some fifty feet away. He touched Cor on the shoulder, pointed the fellow out to her. He felt her nod. She reached to caress the dorfox. When she was satisfied that Ancho was alert and radiating, they resumed their walk. Svir breathed a nearly audible sigh of relief as they passed the sentry unchallenged. They were almost thirty yards past the hallucinated soldier when a low, determined voice spoke from their rear. "Halt. Who goes there?"

Svir froze. Damn. The first sentry was a decoy. At any second the other man might fire. They were lucky he bothered to challenge at all.

"I said 'Who goes there?' Respond or I fire."

Svir gulped and tried to speak. "Erl Bonnip, trying to find the latrine." As he spoke, Cor turned and walked casually toward the voice in the bush. Now that Ancho had noticed the other fellow he was radiating his I'm-not-here. Since the sentry was already alerted, the signal couldn't cover Svir's existence—so he must stand exposed.

"Advance and be recognized."

Svir moved cautiously toward the voice. At best he would be turned back—and that only if the sentry didn't notice the tripod and signaler he was carrying. . . .

There came a dull thunk and a muffled groan. Then a figure he identified as Cor's emerged from the thicket.

"It's okay," she whispered. "I didn't hit him hard, but Ancho gave him a good dose."

"Fine. Let's go." Sometimes Cor acted a good deal more vicious than her mild manner would indicate.

They continued along the trail. The night no longer seemed particularly tranquil. He was beginning to realize that this job was not the little side errand Tatja had made it sound. If they weren't shot by Sfierranyil or Crownesse sentries, there was always the possibility that Rebel infiltrators might be nearby.

The ground sloped down now. Technically they were in the Picchiu River valley. Some seven miles away they could see the forested hills of the other side of the valley. Svir thought he could see the river itself, a narrow silver band occasionally showing through the dense foliage along its bank. The clear, pleasant cooing of a fatbat sounded nearby. How many alert eyes were hidden in this peaceful scene?

The forest thinned, and they could move quickly and quietly. Their first objective was to get far enough away from the camp so that its position wouldn't be given away by their activities. He swore silently. If Tatja were sure of her theory, why bother with such a precaution?

Tatja had gone over the plan in mind-numbing detail during the two-day voyage from Bayfast. Svir was worried. Could she be thinking by wish rather than reason? She seemed certain that an alien mind was involved here. She claimed the alien had somehow been marooned here and so was using native materials and native armies to attain its incomprehensible goals. But what was her evidence?

Now the presumed alien must be contacted, and since this was an operation at cross purposes with the official goal of the Crownesse expeditionary force, he and Cor had to do it in an unofficial way.

He guided Cor into a light thicket. They settled down. He looked into the sky, found the Hourglass, and extended its base to intersect the long bar of the Northern Cross. Now that he had north fixed, he could estimate the azimuth in Tatja's message—the azimuth of the Rebel camp.

As he set the tripod on the ground and screwed the signaler on it, Cor took out paper and pen, ready to record any answer. He rubbed the starting strip and felt the box warm as its fuel burned. He grasped the shutter trip and recalled the exact words Tatja required. The message was in Savoy Mercantile Code—the most common signaling code of Crownesse, but it would mean very little to anyone other than the individual for whom it was intended: AS THE ISLAND APE SAID TO THE SHIPWRECKED SAILOR: MAY I AID YOU? Since island apes are brainless, only a very peculiar person would take the message as code by analogy.

He began tripping out the message. The lamp's shutter flew open and shut with barely audible clicks. The night air was clear, and the box was well shielded, so there was no evidence from his position of the narrow light beam he was casting across the valley. He had barely finished the third word when he saw a flickering yellow point of light appear down by the river. He ignored it and concentrated on his own message. Behind him, Cor whispered the letters she was recording from the other signal lamp: "KZT PMP A PRP TOZRNR F."

He finished the message and folded the tripod. "Let's go. I'll bet you iron that was one of our own spies reporting back that someone was signaling enemy lines from this position. If Profirio doesn't land a shell on us we'll be shot by our own people."

They scrambled out of the brush and trotted across the open ground. Svir dropped the signaler. Without that damning evidence, they could perhaps avoid being shot out of hand. He guided Cor by the waist. She paid little attention to the ground, but kept an anxious face turned toward the river valley. On her shoulder, Ancho made whimpering noises.

Cor stopped, and Svir followed her gaze. Far across the valley, at the top of the far crest, the pinpoint light of a signal lamp winked on and off. Cor took her book out and recorded every letter. The message was short—only two words. The first word was nonsense. Svir wondered if it were simply a military code. He felt Cor shrug. "I think the friend yonder plays Tatja's game—maybe she can translate."

They watched for nearly half a minute, but nothing more was forthcoming. Further up the hill they were stopped by a party of Guards. Ancho was either asleep or afraid, because he didn't radiate anything effective. Svir identified himself as the Astronomer Royal and demanded to be taken to the command area to report a disgraceful breach of security he had noticed.

Less than fifteen minutes later they walked through the light trap of the command tent. Though large and well appointed, the tent had a crudeness that labeled it provincial. A single oil lamp flickered brightly over the scene. Svir and Cor walked past the officers and Guards who stood bleary-eyed behind the generals of Crownesse. In the middle of the tent sat Tatja Grimm. Her face was strangely slack. She glanced up and for a moment didn't seem to recognize them. What had happened? Svir looked at the provincials on the other side of the tent, but there was nothing unusual in their aspect. Apparently she had been talking to the young underofficer who stood on the other side of the table.

Cor handed Svir the notebook. He bowed to Tatja and laid it on the table. She stared at the message for a long moment: JOLLE JESTS. Her slack expression was replaced by a faint smile. She looked up at Svir, then at the fellow standing on the other side of the table. She spoke very softly. "We were wrong, Svir. There are two of them."

Svir looked more carefully at the other man. There was enough silver on his shoulders to make him very high ranking indeed. His chair was set slightly ahead of the other provincial generals. For a moment he returned Svir's gaze with a faint, puzzled frown. Then he smiled and leaned forward. His voice was low. "How many more are there like you three?"

Tatja replied just as softly, "How many more are there like you two?"

"Just we two. You see, I'm a gendarme, a policeman. The thing called Profirio is—a monster."

CHAPTER 12

It was claimed that the Riverside Road in Picchiu Province passed through the most beautiful country in the world. At the moment, Svir could find no fault in the assertion. The road ran straight along the Picchiu River and was surrounded by a young clean forest whose trees often extended their branches to form a roof across the road, a roof that scattered green and gold highlights upon the gray pavement.

They were nearly ten thousand feet above sea level now, and though the air was thin, it seemed wonderfully crisp, dry. For the first time since they had left Bayfast, Svir felt really clean. He and Cor had been with the first party to come down to the river that morning, and had taken a quick swim in the fast, icy waters of the Picchiu.

Even now he could hear the river roll along some feet away. That sound would come louder as they moved upstream, as the valley became a gorge and the river bed sloped more steeply.

It was when the forest roof parted that the most impressive part of the scene was visible. Still miles away, the main peaks of the Doomsday range rose thousands of feet above the road to hulk white against the bright blue sky. Except for a delicate cloud band at the fourteen-thousand-foot level, every detail was visible. Much of the flanks was free of snow, and the bare bones of the young mountains stood black and gray and yellow and brown. Svir thought he could see every crystal-line striation there. In the nearer distance rugged hills ranged on either side of the river valley. Downstream those hills were fairly gentle and covered with the same deciduous forest as the valley proper. But here they were covered with dark-needle looproot tree. And they were fast becoming too rugged even for the looproot—now great sections of naked bedrock were visible. As the valley became a gorge, the hillsides would become cliff faces.

But no matter how formidable the valley walls looked, Svir knew there were small winding footways hidden far above the river. And somewhere up there the enemy's infantry and supply trains made their slow, difficult way. By now those forces were probably several miles behind the combined Crownesse-Sfierranyil army, since the Crown's men were using the wide, straight Riverside Road.

Through the trees bordering the road, Svir could see foot soldiers paralleling the cavalry and art'ry. The Sfierranyil battle groups had been annexed to the Crown battle groups, so now the force had nearly twenty-four thousand men and five hundred art'ry pieces. From his position in the second battle group, Svir couldn't even see the head of the column—some thousand yards ahead. Before and behind him was the line of creaking supply and art'ry wagons, puffing skoats, silent infantrymen. The line stretched out nearly nine miles behind him. It was certainly not the largest force Tatja could field, but the Crown's battle groups were composed of the best men and equipment from the best military organization in the world.

And of all the people marching along this road, only four knew the real reason they were here. Last night he had witnessed the strangest revelation of his life.

Tatja had adjourned the conference in the tent. This had been a relief to most of those present. They had been up all afternoon. Not even Haarm Wechsler had noticed that Tatja and Jolle stayed behind when the others left. Empty, the tent was like a cave. The flickering torch lighted four intent faces, but everything beyond was darkness. There Jolle revealed the secret behind all recorded history. *All the world was a breeding farm. Slaughtering operations would begin as soon as the creature called Profirio regained contact with his superiors.*

There had been a long silence at this. Svir felt himself caught in a nightmare that would disappear if he could only show how implausible it was. He was the first to break the silence. "For food?"

The other shook his head. Svir wondered for a moment if Jolle were his real name. Profirio was certainly an alias, since it had a distinctive Upcoast flavor. "Well, then what *does* he want to kill us for?"

Jolle spoke a single word. "Golems."

Svir looked blank.

Jolle stared at the three of them for a moment. Then he spoke to Tatja. "There's really only one of you, right?"

She nodded. "Yes, and I've looked."

"Tough," Jolle commiserated. He waved at Cor and Svir, and Tatja replied, "Fingers."

"Hmm," said Jolle, "perhaps I should have, too."

"But surrogate pain. Is there?"

"No. Ten trillion. Human too." He nodded. "You're it and foxily burnt."

Tatja smiled shyly.

Svir's jaw dropped. What were they talking about? Occasionally Tatja would carelessly address him in this fashion, but his blank look had always forced her to return to normal speech. Now she had found someone on her own level, and there was no need for "redundancy." He was about to ask for a translation, when Jolle said, "Excuse me Minister Hedrigs, Miss Ascuasenya. If you're going to be in on this, you might as well know what's going on as far as is possible. I had just assumed from the way you worked together that you . . . To answer your question: perhaps golem is not the right word, but what shall I say? Have you ever heard this term?" He made a meaningless sound. "No? Well it was too much to hope that very much Anglic would have survived their processing—especially a term without referent. So I'll use 'golem' to mean thinking machine. If your technology were just fifty years more advanced, you would think you knew exactly what I mean, because you would have constructed primitive golems yourself. As it is I am restrained to the vocabulary of superstition, though perhaps this is for the best, because a word like golem will never give you the false sense of understanding you might have if . . . The golems I refer to are much more like magic than any science you can imagine. Even you, Marget. Until you have training I suggest you accept the magical connotation

I give my story. Then you won't be fooled in false analogies with the thinking machines that you are capable of inventing. . . ."

Jolle's accent was perfect, and he ordered his words properly. Nevertheless his speech was strange. He spoke rapidly, running one sentence into another. If a sentence were especially long, his voice would drop and he would mumble the ending, as if the words were a redundant, painful ritual. His hands never stopped moving. The overall effect was impressive. Svir could imagine how the provincials had been overwhelmed by a man who spewed forth ideas faster than he could even voice them.

Occasionally Tatja sounded like this, though she was perfectly capable of slow, natural exposition—after all, she had grown up here. Was Jolle's manner an affectation, or was he unable to slow down? It had never occurred to Svir that it might be difficult to act stupid.

Jolle continued, "Though they are necessary to the function of our society, golems are expensive to *construct*. There is, however, a relatively cheap—and highly immoral—way of improvising golems. That method is to, hmm, destroy the souls of lesser creatures and so reduce them to golems. Pröfe—Profirio—is in the employ of a misanthropic organization that has spent three thousand years preparing this planet as a cheap golem-production plant. First they chose a planet nearly a thousand light-years from the major centers of our activity. Then they seeded the planet with creatures like you, Minister Hedrigs, creatures they kidnapped from the colonial backwaters of civilization. They destroyed your memories, dumped you here, and waited. My type lives a very long time and can afford to be patient. Every hundred years or so, the organization sent a scout vehicle—crewed by the likes of Profirio—to analyze your population, technology."

"Yes," broke in Tatja. "We have historical records of some of those visits."

"Really?"

"In fact, we observed one of your vehicles enter our system last year."

"You saw my drive stutter. Very surprising. Your technology is further along then than they guessed—or else you were lucky. But that was one of the reasons for these periodic scouting missions. They wanted the planet's population to reach a billion so their operations could be profitable; but even more important, they didn't want you to have even an interplanetary flight technology—that would have meant a drastic increase in the cost of their operations. And essentially their motives are quite understandable: they want a profit. This whole operation is dictated by the principle of least effort for maximum gain."

"What would then happen," asked Cor, "if Profirio were successful?"

"Once he communicates to his superiors that things are ripe for harvest, they will set up a slaughterhouse on that twin planet of yours—Seraph. Three or four percent of your population will be spirited to Seraph for slaughter every year. There is no escape from such abductions, and in fact it will all seem quite supernatural. No alien need land on this world. Technological progress will stop; inventions will disappear, experiments explode. Other than that, the organization will have no interest in what you do. As long as your population growth rate remains constant, the operation will show a profit." He spread his hands in a gesture that seemed to put the prediction in the subjunctive.

"Their plans have come perilously close to success. But no matter how expensive artificial golems may be, and no matter how necessary they are to most of our activities, only a very small fraction of my kind are warped enough to buy golems produced through the slaughter of innocents. My friends and I have known for nearly a thousand years that Profirio's organization was planning something like this, but we didn't know where they were operating. I have spent most of the last four hundred years ingratiating myself to these criminals. Finally my efforts were rewarded. I was hired to accompany Profirio on the present survey of your world.

"My mission was going quite smoothly as we entered your system. We left our vehicle in orbit more than six hundred thousand miles out. Any closer and if you had good telescopes—as it appears you do—you would spot the thing immediately. Then we came down to Tu. We landed in the outback of Sfierranyi Province. I won't go into the gruesome details, but I bobbled my role and Profirio caught on to me. We had quite a fight out there in the hills last summer. I'm a little surprised that the pryotechnics were not observed—but a typhoon was moving inland at the time and I guess everybody was too busy to notice. Our set-to destroyed almost all equipment we had brought down for our survey. Our struggle had to be continued with native resources.

"Our little scout boat is still out there, and the man who communicates with it will be victorious, because our boat can be commanded from a distance. I have one instrument left—it's similar to your signalers. But to use it I must know the exact position of the boat. I need a large telescope to accomplish that. And that's why both Profirio and I have done all the things that you've heard about.

"We both needed excuses to get the native armies to cooperate with us. We are persuasive individuals—but the natives need some excuse, however slim, to provoke them to war. Profirio chose to revolt against your central government. I did the logical thing and led the local militia on a campaign against the Rebels. It is blind luck that it worked out this way—that your forces and mine met as allies. But I apologize for using your army this afternoon to trick Profirio's art'ry into revealing itself.

"Unless you people are hiding something, there are only two large—more than fifty-inch—scopes extant. That's why we had the battle at Kotta-svo-Picchiu. Profirio got there first and was hoping to hold out until dark. I was forced to destroy the scope rather than let him use it. With the Kotta Eye gone, we are forced to go after the High Eye. At the moment, I hold a decisive advantage since we are free to use Riverside Road with impunity and so get to O'rmouth first."

"Excuse me," spoke Svir, "but why did you bother with all these armies? On a good skoat you could have made it to O'rmouth in just a few days. Then you could have applied your powers of persuasion directly to the astronomers."

Tatja didn't let Jolle answer that one. "I think Jolle and Profirio view armies as you might a shirt of nylon armor. If either of them had taken off alone for the Doomsday area, the other might have got control of one of the provinces and then used all of its resources to destroy a single unarmed man. It's a question of balancing the speed with the risk."

"That's right," spoke Jolle. "Eventually, Profirio may be reduced to this sort of personal action, but if so it will be a sign of desperation. I hope he tries it. Then he'll have to try to persuade the Doomsdaymen to cooperate with him rather than us, and his identity will be clearly . . ." Jolle took a deep breath, interrupting his own rushing flow of speech. "One of us will control the High Eye—and the future of this planet will be determined."

CHAPTER 13

The call to dismount brought Svir back to the present. It was late morning, and they had been on the road for more than five hours. It was time to water the skoats. At this point the road moved in close to the Picchiu River and there was a stretch of some three hundred yards where it was possible to bring the animals down to the water.

He and Cor scrambled off their mounts and waited for further directions. Water call was conducted with more precision and ceremony than most supply functions. He had read somewhere that the efficiency of a mounted command could be measured by observing water call. He had to admit that watering twelve thousand animals was not simple—especially when those animals had a tendency to herd and were generally skittish.

Finally it came time for their battle group to go to the river. The art'ry skoats were released from their gun carriages, and the animals and men moved over the rocky ground toward the river. Behind them gun crews loaded their weapons and received fire control directions. Then came the concussive *crump, crumpcrump* as the battery lofted six-inch shells into the sky. Ten miles downstream those shells would tear craters in the road the army had so recently traversed. It was judged that the time required for the enemy to get his artillery around those broken places in the road would easily keep him from ever getting within range of the Crown's Men. Too bad about the road. The expeditionary force had already stopped five caravans bound for the coast—caravans carrying hundreds of ounces of copper and iron from O'rmouth. Such interference with Doomsday commerce was not going to win the Crown any friends, but Tatja intended to stay ahead of the news of her vandalism.

The Picchiu River was nearly one hundred yards wide at this point. The water foamed and showered as it moved through the rapids. Only a small canoe could have navigated that torrent. Quartermasters had assembled several hundred watering troughs, since the water directly from the river was much too cold for the animals. The skoats had to be urged to the troughs, but when they began drinking, it was with characteristic greediness. Svir examined the animals critically. It was amazing how much they had changed in just two or three days. They were no longer sleek and furry. Now their bodies were covered with superficial cuts and gashes. In spite of the fact that they were fed four times a day, their tendons and bones showed clearly through their skin. He commented on this to Cor.

"Yes, I know," she responded in a subdued voice. "On the fastboats I wondered why the harnesses and the collars were small for the animals they were assigned to. Now I know. This march burns the flesh from them. Most of the collars are now actually too big for the creatures. You know, we lost thirty of them in the artillery attack—but three times that many have died from exhaustion. See—" She pointed at a quartermaster veterinarian. The fellow walked slowly down the rank of skoats, lifting their blankets and painting antiseptic on the raw sores and cuts he found. The Loyalists' animals were in much poorer shape than the Crown's skoats—they had been in the campaign five times as long. Even with all the quartermaster's care, this was still killing work. By the time he reached the end of the watering line, the vet had marked three skoats to be dropped from the train. Those animals were in no shape to continue with the expedition even as unburdened reserve.

Svir felt his wife's arm close around his. "This makes

me a little sick." Her voice sounded choked. "For no fault of their own and for no gain of their own, they lose their lives."

He discovered suddenly that he felt the same way—though really it was irrational. Animals are slaughtered for food, for leather. Here, too, they were doing something useful. And they were not being intentionally mistreated. But he didn't voice these thoughts to Cor, and for the first time he felt affection for the poor animal that had carried him so far.

For most of the men this was a rest stop. Behind the skoats the men of the battle group lay or sat on the ground. Most of the Provincial Loyalists lay motionless on the ground. The Loyalists never had been anything but part time militiamen, and they had been in the campaign for nearly forty days. The militia uniforms were of poor materials. Many of their boots were held together with ragged cloth bands. In some cases, blood and pus oozed through broken leather to discolor the cloths. The Crownesse troops had better equipment and were fresh—besides, they were trained for this sort of thing. They kept apart from their unprofessional counterparts. But even with the professionals, there was evidence of strain. There was little of the good-natured talk of earlier rest stops.

The hospital wagon arrived with the last ranks of the battle group. Since they were moving through nearly wild lands, the Crown's Men were forced to carry their casualties with them—at least so long as those casualties weren't too numerous. At present there were probably a hundred wounded—and about twelve in this battle group. The hospital wagon had its cloth sides rolled up so that the occupants were exposed to the open air. Svir found it difficult to look away from that wagon. There was nothing repulsive about the interior—no gore. Everything seemed quite clean and comfortable. Some of the patients were even sitting up, and these looked better than most of the "ready" troops. But others in the wagon lay quite still, with only their heads exposed. They might have been corpses except for the trouble the Crown was taking to bring them along.

Two medics moved to the back of the wagon and drew one of those long white forms off the platform. They carried it around to the far side of the wagon. A colonel and three enlisted men with entrenching tools followed the medics into the brush. Svir recalled that a field grade officer was required to participate in the burial of all combat victims. He glanced at the skoats as they stood at the watering trough. He remembered Cor's comment that these creatures were dying for a cause alien to them. He looked back at the soldiers and militiamen, and her comment seemed just as true there.

"Don't think fuzzy, Svir." The voice came from behind them. Svir felt Cor start with surprise. He turned and saw Tatja. Instead of her usual camouflage uniform, she wore a feminine outfit which wouldn't have been out of place in Bayfast—but which here seemed as appropriate as a jester at an execution. The oppression that clouded everyone's mind did not touch her. Never before had she seemed quite so callous to the problems of the people she used.

"What's fuzzy about it?" he answered angrily, without bothering to wonder whether they were talking about the same thing. Tatja had a talent for guessing what was eating at people.

"Most wars are not caused by the evil machinations of a few. You probably have some idea that these poor people would live in peace if left to themselves. I'm saying that in general that isn't true. If you study history you'll find plenty of wars that occurred because the *people* saw that some personal advantage would devolve to themselves through victory. I imagine that most Sfierranyii figure that their support of the Crown will get them a portion of Picchiul lands after the war. Many of these militiamen thought they would win booty in this adventure—though I doubt they feel that way now."

"Hell, Tatja, so what? We're not talking about the general case. If it weren't for your kind, we *would* have peace."

Tatja smiled. "It's true that Jolle and I are manipulating everyone. But don't forget the true reason for all this. Our men and the militia believe they die for a cause that we know is trivial, but in the final analysis, this war is more important and more just than any in the history of this planet. If we fail, the future of all the people in the world will be much darker than any war could make it."

She had him there. The sacrifice was certainly necessary—even if the people who made the sacrifice were ignorant of the ultimate justification. But he wondered if this argument would be so appealing if he were one of those who were going to get cut to pieces.

Now the skoats were being led from the troughs. Some squads were already being assembled. Soon the next battle group would arrive. The art'ry fire had stopped, and now the officers' voices seemed loud. Of course no one came near Cor and Svir and Tatja. Unless the Queen wished otherwise, she had privacy—even when she walked about in the open.

Cor spoke. "But Marget, how do you know that you aren't also being used?"

"What?" Tatja seemed nonplussed, but Svir had the sudden feeling that his wife had uncovered a bombshell.

"Why should we believe the story of the monster and the gendarme? Grant the story, how do we know that Jolle, rather than Profirio, is the gendarme?" The bombshell detonated with soundless violence in Svir's mind. "Wouldn't the criminal tell us the same story as the one who tries to save us?" Cor finished.

Tatja shrugged. "I suppose so. But there is no way we can test the story except by sitting tight and watching things develop. Besides"—and now she was smiling again, the same silly grin—"in view of my past successes, I trust my judgment and intuition much more than I trust yours." She looked around, evidently dismissing the problem. "You better get your mounts. This battle group is moving out and I want you to stay with it." She turned and walked toward the command wagon of the next battle group, which was just then creaking into the clearing. In her short skirt and lacy blouse she might have been at a picnic instead of a war.

What had happened to Tatja? For the first time in nearly five years, he didn't have a friend who had all the angles figured, who could solve virtually any problem. He looked at Cor, and saw on her face the same look of quiet tension he felt on his own. They were confronted with a life-and-death problem—and if they didn't solve it, no superior being was going to save them. There was a monster loose, and somehow they must discover who it was.

CHAPTER 14

The sun was halfway to the horizon when they made their move. Svir sat up and pushed aside the insect netting which hung over their sleeping cots. The loud, unwavering hum of a three year cicada was an overpowering soporific. The sunlight was no fainter than in the morning, but the afternoon was a time to sleep and the commanders of the expedition had finally recognized that fact (or perhaps it was simply that now they could move as easily along the Riverside Road by night as by day, so it was possible to permit a reasonable sleep schedule).

No human sounds could be heard: apparently the sentries were keeping static positions, as was usual with day bivouac. But all around them were the insect and bat sounds, and the river burbled in the near distance. Pink flowers crowded between the leaf needles of the looproot above them, and the scent was nearly overpowering in such concentration. Through gaps between the branches he could see the walls of the river gorge rise thousands of feet overhead. They had nearly reached the mouth of the glacier. O'rmouth was hidden beyond the northern wall, above the glacier. The gorge was so deep now that they couldn't see He'gate's summit—their ultimate goal. Near the top of the gorge Svir saw a broadwing daybat soaring lazily back and forth across the updrafts as it scanned the ground with its sharp eyes, watching for its prey.

Cor sat up. "Ready?" he whispered. She nodded. "Now remember how we're going to play this. I think we'll be safe even if we're discovered. The key is to have Tatja nearby—so Jolle can't kill us without her knowing it. You're going to go to her tent while I take Ancho to Jolle's wagon. I've got a noise bomb. If you hear it, bring Tatja as fast as you can—I may still be in one piece."

This recapitulation was needless, but it put off action for a few more seconds.

She squeezed his arm. "It'll go all right."

"Yeah." He grimaced. "After all you aren't taking any of the risks."

Her eyes widened in consternation at these half-serious words. "I . . . I'll go to Jolle's wagon instead, if you want. After all, I can handle Ancho better than you."

He blushed. Cor meant it; she wasn't trying to shame him. And knowing her sincerity, he felt truly ashamed. "Never mind, honey. I was just kidding. C'mon."

They stood beside their cots and looked about. Svir felt a little faint. They were nearly twelve thousand feet above sea level, and he was learning first hand the symptoms of hypoxia. The only good thing about the altitude was that even in the middle of the afternoon it was not particularly hot.

As they walked through the looproot grove, Ancho scrambled back and forth across Svir's shoulders. The little animal was normally most active at this time of day, and for once his large friends weren't trying to make him keep still so they could sleep.

During the day, security was less strict than at night. Unless they tried to give away the bivouac's position to the enemy, they would probably not even be challenged.

They parted. Cor took the path that led to Tatja's tent, as Svir walked toward the provincial headquarters area. Now the thick gray arches of the looproot were more closely set, and in places the branches and needle leaves above the roots reduced the sunlight to a gray-green twilight. Here the underbrush was shaded out. Tents and cots were scattered at random through darker portions of the grove. The scene was quite different from the display bivouacs he had seen back in Crownesse, where tents and vehicles were set in pretty rectangular formations that looked so neat and military.

The moment he left Cor, he began working on Ancho. It seemed that as the years went by the animal became better and better at responding to the tactile instructions of his masters, and Svir was pretty confident that Ancho would not fail him now. The first sentry that they passed came to attention and saluted. Good. The sentry probably identified him as Jolle. Fifteen feet ahead, the grove thinned and sunlight flooded a brush-covered clearing. Parked at the edge of the clearing was the camouflaged hulk of Jolle's wagon. The wagon's tent had been pulled out and assembled. If Jolle were in the tent, would it rupture the sentries' credulity when another Jolle appeared outside the tent? . . . He would know in a moment.

He walked briskly toward the wagon's rear entrance. The guards around the wagon saluted. No one attempted to stop him. He had been identified as Jolle again. He walked purposefully to the little doorway. The entrance had a standard leverlatch. He pulled at the latch. It didn't budge. He pulled again, harder. He found himself sweating as he wondered what the sentries thought of his inability to enter "his own" wagon. Perhaps one of the guards had a key, but he didn't dare ask. Besides, he noticed on closer inspection that no lock mechanism was visible. He had no chance of getting in here.

He leaned against the side of the wagon and pretended to admire the tree flowers that drooped heavily from the looproot branches that sheltered the wagon from snoopers further up the gorge. There was only one other place he could try: the tent entrance. Jolle probably wasn't there; but if he were, he might react so abruptly that Svir wouldn't be able to set off the noise bomb that would bring Cor and Tatja.

Well, he had come this far; it seemed ridiculous to back out now. He reflected with some irritation that in general his courage derived from the fear that he might be taken for a coward. He walked to the tent at the other end of the wagon. The vents were open, but it was too dark within for him to see anything. The guard at the entrance saluted, addressed him as Jolle.

He took a deep breath and decided to commit himself. "I'm going to be in and out all afternoon. I don't wish to be disturbed." That might help take care of inconsistencies in the sentry's mind if he later saw the real Jolle outside the tent.

"Very good, sir," the sentry replied.

Svir pulled back the entrance curtain and stepped into the dimness. All was quiet. It was warm, but not hot. There was even a faint breeze. The rectangular vents admitted the sunlight onto the carpeted floor, and after a few seconds he could see the interior in detail. No one else was present. The room was lavishly appointed. Apparently Jolle had a penchant for the good life. From one corner came the pleasant odor of burning perfume. Beside the tent mast stood a low, luxuriously upholstered couch and a table supporting a coolchest and bottles of drink.

He moved swiftly across the room, toward the entrance of the wagon itself. The deep carpet made his movements silent: the loudest sounds to be heard were Ancho's breathing and the cry of a daybat outside. Even in the dimness, he could see that this entrance was different from the one at the rear. When the troops were in march the tent was stowed in the front of the wagon, behind a pair of clamshell doors which now stood open. Beyond these doors was the entrance to the interior of the wagon. A beautifully painted partition of fine-weave spider silk stretched taut from one side of the wagon to the other. The doorway was mounted at the center of the partition. The spider silk was so fine that Svir would be clearly visible to anyone behind the partition.

He reached forward and pulled at the leverlatch on the little door. This one didn't move either. And again there was no evidence of a locking mechanism. The only explanation was that the door was barred from the inside. But this would imply that there *was* someone in there. What now?

His fear eased for an instant as he heard Tatja's voice outside the tent. But Jolle was with her. They were coming into the tent. Even now Jolle was telling the sentry at the entrance to move away—that secret matters were to be discussed. Svir stood frozen for a moment, and Ancho echoed his discomfort, whimpering where he crouched on the astronomer's shoulder. Svir's only chance was to hide and hope that the dorfox would give him some protection with his I'm-not-here signal. If Jolle were like Tatja it was indeed a slim hope, but Ancho might be able to dull the godlings' senses to merely human levels. He ducked behind the ornate stand that supported the bowl of burning perfume. The stand was directly in front of the locked doorway to the interior of the wagon.

He had barely succeeded in making Ancho change

the illusion he broadcast when Tatja and Jolle entered the tent. He couldn't risk looking around the corner of the stand. He held his breath and waited to be discovered. Although the perfume was pleasant in small doses, in high concentrations it brought a nearly overpowering desire to sneeze. He heard them sit on the low couch, and wondered how the interior of the tent could ever have seemed dim. The sunlight coming down from the ceiling vents splashed over the intricately worked blue-green rug. His footprints might still be visibly impressed in that pile.

"Really feral?" Tatja's soft voice came from the area of the couch.

"No. 'Sport' is more accurate." Jolle's voice sounded perfectly calm. Perhaps he hadn't been detected. On impulse, he reached behind him and pulled again at the leverlatch of the interior door. It moved smoothly downward and the door swung open. Svir came close to squeaking his surprise. He looked through the little doorway, but no one was visible in the darkness beyond. Now he had another unpleasant choice: he could remain behind the perfume stand or he could sneak up through that doorway into the wagon. If he moved quickly and quietly, he could probably make it, since the doorway was hidden from the couch by the high perfume stand. And presumably Tatja and Jolle were facing the other way. He would never have dared it without Ancho. Ordinarily Tatja seemed able to hear the faintest sounds. Without the dorfox broadcasting a signal that would put a battle group out of action, she—and probably Jolle—could have heard his heart beating. But in the final analysis it was—surprisingly—his curiosity that decided him.

He turned, slipped up to the entrance, pulled himself through, and quietly shut the door. No alarms sounded. Except for the blood singing in his ears, he could hear no sound in the dark interior of the wagon. The spider silk screen now provided an almost transparent window on the more brightly lit tent area. Tatja and Jolle were sitting on the couch, and were facing almost directly away from him. There was no sign that he had been discovered. He felt Ancho purring against the side of his neck as the little animal continued to broadcast deception.

Tatja was dressed even more gushily than that morning.

A party shawl of virtually transparent silk covered her shoulders. Svir could see the top of her low-cut, finely embroidered blouse. Jolle wore his usual black militia uniform. He was pouring drinks. Svir pulled his attention away from the tent and inspected the wagon. It was hot, poorly ventilated. Except for the perfume drifting through the silk screen, no odors were apparent. And it wasn't completely dark. Along the length of the wagon, red and orange prisms had been set in the roof, and a dim, hellish light filtered through them onto the contents of the wagon. Everything seemed jumbled. Along one side of the curving wall were the reddish hulks of a bed and bath. The rest of the room was filled with books and ornately carved cabinets. The room seemed more like a wizard's den than the quarters of a man from the stars. It was hard to believe that just twenty inches away the sun was shining, bats were flying, and red flowers were scattering blue-gold mist through cool mountain air.

Svir looked back through the silk screen. Jolle handed Tatja a goblet of clear wine. They sipped in silence. Then Jolle spoke. "It was sloppy language. But"—he waved broadly—"we're all the same species. They just don't have the benefit of technology."

"Natural state?" Tatja sounded incredulous.

"Sure. My parents even. No. Call it magic."

"Please?"

Jolle laughed sympathetically at the pleading tone in her voice. He reached out to caress the smooth, clear skin of her neck. She moved closer, and even through the silk screen she seemed dazed.

"Well," replied the alien, "I can try. But it will just mislead you. You're asking for an education, not an explanation. There's drugs, genetic manipulation, and direct amplification. The last was first because it's easiest—but the deadliest, as the first ones discovered."

Svir followed every word closely. He was almost onto what they were talking about. When he filled in the blanks, it made sense.

"Why deadly?" she asked.

"Last last, please," he answered, and extended his arms around her shoulders, drew her against his chest. She came slowly but without reluctance. Her body had none of the tension that was her usual armor.

Now Jolle's voice was low, barely audible. His black hair mixed with Tatja's red. "First first: what's a natural definition of information?"

"Hmm." Tatja seemed half asleep, but after a moment of thought her voice came muffled against Jolle's chest. "Something like the information in a signal is the log of the inverse of the probability of the signal."

"That's okay. The next conclusion you have to reach is about the problem of redundancy. It's possible to reduce error in a communication link to arbitrarily low levels with fixed redundancy. See that?"

A long silence. She appeared more interested in his neck than the question. Finally her voice came, so low pitched it hardly seemed her own. She was obviously thinking of more important things. "Yes, though it's more complicated than that. I never thought about that before. . . ."

Svir came near groaning aloud. The conversation had passed beyond intelligibility just when he thought he might be able to follow it. He looked at the door that had opened so conveniently for him. Perhaps there was some clue as to why it had done so. There was. The door could be locked from the inside by a heavy wooden bar. In a way this was ridiculous, since anyone with a sharp knife could have cut through the silk screen. On the other hand, when the tent was not set up, there was probably a wooden panel fitted over the screen. One end of the bar was enclosed in metallic collar—an expensive and wasteful ornament. Touching this collar was an (iron?) bar. Around the bar were wound several hundred turns of yellow wire sheathed in some transparent resin. There was a fortune in metals here—to what purpose? The wires led away from the bar toward a large wood chest on the floor beside the bed. If he were going to search the wagon, this was the place to start.

He glanced back through the silk screen. The high-powered conversation was over. He couldn't see Tatja at all, but now her blouse was draped over the back of the couch. He looked away from the screen, blushing. Being a snoop in a good cause didn't hurt his conscience, but voyeurism was a little out of his league. It was obvious now why Tatja was so dense when it came to discussing the possibility that Jolle was a bastard. When a goddess is in love, she's just as irrational as anyone else. Even the argument that there were whole worlds of people who were her equals would probably have no effect now that she had fallen for this man.

Svir turned and followed the yellow wires to the armoire. The chest was an expensive Sdan piece. He felt the ghoulish hardwood faces, hunting for the tongue catch that the Sdan carpenters worked into their designs. He heard a faint insect buzzing near the box, but in the dim light he couldn't see the bug that was making the noise. His searching fingers found the catch and the lid of the cabinet came up with silent, counterbalanced precision

A blue glow radiated from that opening. For an instant he was frozen by the flickering, almost actinic gleam. He leaned forward to inspect the interior. His first impression was that the box was filled with treasure—large, glowing, blue and green jewels. The colors and intensities were constantly changing, so that it was hard to define the exact size and shape of the jewels. Along the inside wall of the box were a number of silvery boxes. In the shifting reflections they seemed almost transparent. After his eyes became accustomed to the sight, he noticed that the copper wires he had followed from the wagon door were connected to one of those little boxes. He looked deep into the pile of "jewels." Though they were motionless, the changing colors made the pile shimmer and appear to flow like foam onto an island shore.

The buzzing sound was louder now. An alarm! The buzz reached a crescendo and became a screeching, inhuman wail. "Master! Help me! I will be stolen!" From the tent, he heard Tatja's surprised exclamation and the sounds of rapid motion. Without thinking, he ran through the reddish dimness to the other end of the wagon. From the inside it was easy to flip the crossbar out of the way and thrust the door open. As he plunged through the doorway into the blinding sunlight, he heard Jolle enter the wagon.

By luck Svir landed on his feet. As he fell forward, he dug his long legs into the ground and sprinted away. Ancho clung to his shoulder and radiated for all he was worth. The nearest guards were more than forty feet away. They knew something strange was happening, but Ancho's efforts kept them from taking effective action. Even so, a couple of crossbow bolts zipped by him as he fled into the forest. He could hear no pursuers. Apparently Jolle was still in the wagon, inspecting his—slave?

Soon he was deep within the grove, and the looproots formed a long arched hallway around him. Only dim and shifting pencils of light penetrated the branches and leaf needles above. The ground was covered with a deep, resilient layer of white fungus. The shouting behind him had faded. He was still in the bivouac area—that was more than two thousand feet across—and could see occasional tents and wagons. Ancho protected him from the sentries. It took him fifteen minutes to circle back to his own sleeping area.

Now he moved cautiously. If Jolle had identified him, there would be a welcoming committee here. He stayed in the forest shadows and looked out at the sun-dappled cots. Cor was lying on her cot—next to someone else! He did a double take, and examined the figure beside her It didn't move. In fact, its face was a brown piece of cloth.

A dummy, he thought. Good girl! When she discovered that Tatja was going with Jolle to his tent, she had done the only thing possible—return to their sleeping area and construct an alibi. He moved rapidly out of the shadows, pulled the netting aside, and lay down beside his wife. She jerked with surprise. Her hands were clenched white, and there were tears on her cheeks. Together they disassembled the crude dummy, and Svir told her what he had just seen.

Cor burrowed into his arms, her ingenuity gone now that she had someone to depend on. "He'll kill us, Svir. And if we run he'll be sure to catch us. We've got to talk to Tatja."

Svir felt the same panic. They needed protection. But he said, "We can't talk to her yet. She's probably still with Jolle. And—she's not herself. You remember this morning. We'll have to wait until we can get her alone."

Cor whimpered something unintelligible. He tried to comfort her. "I don't think that Jolle saw me. We'll be safe as long as we play innocent." Ancho wormed his way between them, and Svir petted him. There was really nothing more to say.

CHAPTER 15

"Observer Reynolt, we understand all this. I have no desire to hold your lands under my direct control." The Tatja that spoke was the Tatja of old: composed, persuasive, tactful. She had made no attempt to use her ostensible position as the absolute ruler of all The Continent to overawe the Doomsdayman confronting her.

And every bit of her diplomacy would be required to mollify the angry Doomsday priest. In the starlit darkness his triple-pointed mitre made him appear a seven-foot obelisk rather than a human being. He spoke with the sarcastic servility of a subordinate who thinks he has the upper hand. "Your Majesty must know that we Doo'd'en would never ascribe such ill motives to Your Sacred Person. But in our considerable ignorance, we beg to know why you destroyed segments of the Riverside Road, why you razed Kotta-svo-Picchiu, why you destroyed the sacred eye there, and why you now set a vast army on the farmlands beneath our capital."

Tatja was a vague shadow by the low field table, but her voice was clear and distinct. "Observer, for all four incursions we tender our apologies, and for the first three we offer reparations. However, when you understand the situation, I believe you will thank us. You reprove us for acts of war, committed to protect the most holy places of your lands from the Rebel army, which even now masses below us. Do you realize what will happen if the Rebels are not defeated? They are the ones who first invaded your territories. They are the ones who desecrated the Kotta Eye before it was destroyed. Though I cannot present proof now, the Rebels' ultimate goal is the destruction of the High Eye itself."

The priest had no immediate answer to this. There was

the sound of fabric on fabric as he moved to the windowhole of the abandoned stone farmhouse. Observer Reynolt looked futilely into the night. He'gate's dark peak cut a wide bite from the starry sky. Somewhere up there was O'rmouth, capital of Doomsday, and thousands of feet above that, the observatory itself. Two thousand feet below the farmhouse was the Picchiu River, and the mouth of the glacier that fed it. And somewhere down there were twenty-three thousand Loyalists and an unknown number of Rebels.

The Crown's generals stood uneasily in the hovel. In one corner Haarm Wechsler whispered with indignant intensity to Imar Stark, the Crown's chief of staff.

The military felt that the Doomsdaymen should not be cajoled. If these provincials refused to fight for their Queen, they should be ignored until after the battle, and then dealt with as traitors. It seemed a waste of time to stand here debating while the opposing armies were taking their positions. And it seemed doubly strange to the Crown's generals that a militia leader should be in charge of that deployment. At that moment Jolle and the lower staff officers were somewhere down there in the darkness, deploying crossbow men, ground obstacles, FAOs, and art'ry pieces. Soon there would be nothing quiet about the night.

Finally Observer Reynolt spoke. Some of the false servility was gone from his voice. "Yes, Marget, we realize this. We are very unhappy about the situation: you have caused us as much damage as the Rebels. But in the past you have been just and have truly protected us. What aid do you require? Your army—if our reports are accurate—is much larger than any trained force we Doo'd'en could field. And we have none of the bomb throwers which both you and the Rebels have."

Tatja laughed softly. "My troops are great. They can whip four times their number—at sea level. But now we're at fourteen thousand feet. I am sure you understand—even if my own advisors do not—that at these altitudes the efficiency of unacclimated troops deteriorates. My forces already hold decisive advantages—high ground, artillery superiority. But to be sure of victory I want two or three thousand Doomsday fighting men, uh, Celestial Servants." She turned to her chief of staff. "How much time do we have, Immy?"

"The Provincial reported twenty minutes ago that the Rebels probably won't be in position for another five hours. Twilight begins about seven-thirty this morning, so we can expect engagement in five to seven hours."

"Observer Reynolt, it is now forty-thirty," she said. "Can you get a battle group of Celestial Servants into my command by four-thirty?"

"Marget, permit me to signal O'rmouth. My superiors will no doubt approve. The servants will be at your disposal in less than an hour."

The priest gave a shallow bow which was somehow more respectful than the extravagant obeisance he had done earlier.

At this point the generals moved in to discuss the details of the deployment. Strangely, Tatja made no move to dominate or even to participate in the conversation.

Soon she left the small stone building. Cor and Svir followed her. The newly ploughed field outside was steeply sloping, and several times Svir nearly wrenched his foot in the narrow furrows. Ancho held tight to his neck. He had never imagined that ground this rough could be cultivated. Even though terraced, the fields had thirty-degree slopes. Only the hardiest vegetation could survive at these altitudes and in this soil.

Tatja stopped at the edge of the terrace and sat down. Svir felt Cor clutch his elbow with almost painful tension. They walked over to join Tatja. It was obvious that Cor was as unhappy about this confrontation as he was. Unconsciously she was trying to pull him back from the literal and figurative precipice they were approaching.

Tatja's voice floated through the darkness. "Sit down, Svir." They sat. "What do you think of the situation?"

For a second his throat was frozen. Here was the perfect opportunity to bring up what he had seen that afternoon in Jolle's wagon. Tatja was alert now, no longer the soft, yielding woman she had been earlier with Jolle. That was obvious from the way she had just handled the Doomsday priest. From the sound of her movements it seemed that she had gone back to sensible combat dress. He would never have a better chance to try to convince her of Jolle's real objectives. In fact, he might never have another chance. If Profirio were destroyed this night, which seemed likely, Jolle would be left unopposed, and would have no further need of Tatja. But these thoughts only increased his nervousness. For he also remembered what he had seen in the tent. Tatja had finally gotten what she wanted. How could he possibly persuade her to give Jolle up?

The silence stretched on for an endless moment. Finally it was Cor who answered the Queen's question in a voice a bit too high and forced to be natural. "I thought it was really something of a masterstroke, that of convincing the priest to let us use his men."

Tatja laughed for the second time that night. "No, just the natural thing to do. And he really had to do what we asked. They know Profirio has caused much of the damage. And I am their protector. Too bad they're such a bunch of fanatics. I wonder what their reaction will be when they find out that my side intends to desecrate the High Eye with our presence. I can just imagine their scream of 'Betrayal'."

"But Marget," said Svir, puzzled. "You already said that we are poor fighters, even at fifteen thousand feet. We'll be much worse at O'rmouth, and the observatory is nearly ten thousand feet above that. How can you expect success there?"

"You'll see. I assure you, there will be nothing subtle about it. Jolle and I are sure it will work. In the meantime, though, we have a competent adversary down there below us. I'd give a lot to know what *he* is planning."

So the conversation was back to that. He must speak now, Svir realized. Jolle would soon return from the front lines, and then it would be impossible to bring the matter up. Even if the alien didn't kill them before they could finish the story, he could certainly persuade Tatja that it was a fabrication.

With each attempt to speak Svir came closer to actual sound. He couldn't see Tatja well in the dark, but he thought she was looking at him curiously. Finally he managed to hold his fears at bay long enough to let his mouth make the sounds he had been rehearsing for the last half hour. The effect was strange—like listening to someone else talking, or like remembering a previous conversation.

"Tatja, you remember our talk yesterday morning at the watering stop?"

"Uh-huh."

He didn't lose his stride. "We brought up the possibility that perhaps Jolle was lying, Profirio was the gendarme, and Jolle the criminal."

"Yes, I remember all that." There was good humor in her voice, but he could only hope that it expressed sympathy and intelligence rather than the euphoric dullness with which she had greeted this suggestion before.

"You pointed out that we had to wait and watch. Well, Cor and I . . . uh . . . we thought that the situation was so dangerous that perhaps there was something more that could and should be done. If Jolle were the evil one, then there might be some chance that he had lied about the amount of equipment that he had managed to salvage from his fight with the other one, Profirio. In fact it might even be that if these thinking machines are so popular and if Jolle worked for an organization that made use of . . . uh . . . slaughtered humans, then he might even have one with him." There could be no more evasion. If he didn't say it now, she would get ahead of him.

"Marget, this is exactly what I discovered. Jolle *is* the criminal. He has a golem with . . ."

"You were the one in the wagon." The intensity of her accusation was as great as he had feared.

"Y-yes. But I had to, Tatja. We know now that Jolle is the slaver. His golem can even talk, and no ma—"

"You peeping bastard, I'll teach—" In the darkness he had no warning. The lower right side of his face went numb and splinters of pain spread through his head. Simultaneously her other fist buried itself in his middle. Even the nylon webbing of his shrap vest could not protect him from the ramming force of her blow. It bowled him over the edge of the terrace and he began to tumble down the slope. Ancho went flying off into space as Tatja struck him another glancing blow across the head. He lost consciousness.

Tiny yellow points of light floated lazily before his eyes. After a moment of disorientation, he realized he was lying at the base of the terrace slope. Above him he heard Tatja and Cor begin to scramble down toward where he was lying. Cor was screaming at Tatja. There was a *thunk* and her cries were cut off. Cor! He coughed back the blood in his mouth and tried to concentrate on moving toward their sounds. If they could survive just a few seconds, Tatja would cool off.

From across the terrace he heard the sounds of several men moving through the darkness. One of them was running. Running? In the dark? The footsteps stopped, strong hands lifted him to his feet, and Jolle's calm voice sounded in his ear. "Say friend, what's your problem?"

CHAPTER 16

Svir came to lying on rough, lumpy ground, his head pillowed on something soft. When he opened his eyes, he saw Cor looking down at him. His head was in her lap. She smiled as she saw he had come back. A medic walked up and flashed a tiny yellow light in his eyes. He squinted, croaked, "Get that thing away from me." The speech made him aware of the bloody and painful condition of his mouth. His searching tongue discovered two gaps in the teeth of his lower jaw.

"He'll probably be all right. I'll look at him again after the engagement. I think he may have a mild concussion," the medic whispered to Cor.

She nodded and the medic walked away, disappearing beyond a heavy curtain of quilted nylon that hung across the end of the bunker. Svir looked around, dazed.

Though the bunker had been hastily and crudely constructed, it was an effective job. The Crown's Engineers had used a cleft in the terracing. It had been a simple matter to fill the open end with dirt-packed bags and to construct a roof of timber covered with three or four feet of dirt. The occupants of the bunker could survive all but a direct hit with a six-inch shell. Since the enemy was supposed to be without six-inch guns, the bunker should be quite safe unless it was overrun. There was no real floor to the room, just the curving rocky surface of the cleft. Despite the primitive aspect of the chamber, it was obviously a command post. A field table had been set in the middle of the chamber, and on it were detailed maps and overlays of the area. From the roof over the table hung a peculiar lamp that looked very much like the algae pots used in luxury quarters back in Crownesse and on the Islands. Its cool blue radiance lit the maps and the men standing around them. Underofficers moved back and forth through the nearer curtain. They were bringing information that was immediately posted on the overlays. Runners occasionally departed through the far curtain, the one the medic had used.

In his dazed state, Svir absorbed most of this without curiosity; but as the seconds passed, his emotions and memory caught up with events, and he was both frightened and puzzled. The strange light, for instance. Algae pots were terribly hard to keep alive this far from resupply. Why not use an oil lamp? At night no smoke would be visible to give away their location.

He looked up at his wife and whispered, "Why are we here?"

She now looked just as confused as he. "*Nou che,* Svir. I thought Jolle would kill us when he found us with Tatja like that. But he calmed her down, and then had you carried here. I don't know what he's planning, but—"

At that moment the subject of their conversation pulled back the nearer curtain and stepped into the room. In the dim light his face was shadowed, his black hair glinted metallically. He nodded casually to Svir and walked to the map table. There they could see his features more clearly. He seemed relaxed—as Tatja did in such situations. His uniform looked freshly pressed. To him, the officers at the table might have been discussing party plans.

Jolle addressed Imar Stark. "We just received a signal from Marget. She is at her command post and plans are completed there. Our position is to be the prime command post unless it be knocked out by enemy action. As she mentioned before in your presence, she has delegated immediate command of all operations to me. You may check this reading of her message with your own signalman." He nodded at the curtain.

Stark nodded stiffly. He obviously had no love for the situation, but the Queen had been explicit, and besides, this bearded provincial hadn't tried to control the minutiae of combat preparation with the same prickliness that Marget often did.

Jolle continued. "I am putting the militia under you. My generals have already agreed to that—since you are my subordinate in this matter. If our scouts are to be believed—and I suspect some of the signal reports are fakes—the enemy is in position below us. I am saving my artillery until they mass to overrun some point. When that happens, we'll use the plan discussed before." He glanced at the map. "Good. I didn't know the Celestial Servants were in position. General Stark, we can expect engagement at any moment."

"Yes sir." The old military man didn't salute, but his voice was firm and even respectful. The alien turned, and then walked to the curtain. As if by an afterthought, he glanced at Svir. "I'd like to talk with you for a moment, please."

His words were mild, but they brought a chill to Svir's spine. Tatja was deadly when she was merely blindly angry, but this creature was calculating. If he wished them death, then he and Cor would die.

Jolle appeared to mistake the reason for Svir's immobility. He spoke to the men at the table. "Carry the Astronomer Royal in there." He gestured beyond the curtain. "He's had a bad smash, and I don't think he ought to walk."

Svir was gently lifted and carried toward the curtain. He was too confused to notice that Haarm Wechsler was his head porter. The security man had been virtually superfluous on this expedition, and though he was still admitted to command areas, his responsibilities had been reduced to menial tasks.

Beyond the curtain it was completely dark. The men laid him on a low bench and left. No light escaped from the map room as they moved through the curtain. The cloth was thick and layered double to prevent light leaks. Cor sat down by his head. There was a long silence. The wall beside him was dirtpacked bags. He realized there were slit windows at about chest level. The wall was so thick that he couldn't see the sky from his prone position. There was only a gray glow and a faint breeze to indicate the night outside. Jolle stood by the windows for a moment and said nothing. From breathing sounds, Svir realized there was at least one other person in the cool darkness, probably behind Cor. He listened carefully, but all he heard now was a fatbat cooing in the distance. At these altitudes even insects were rare and the night silence was profound. The sounds of people talking could be heard for miles, unless precautions were taken. It was even conceivable that the conversation Tatja had had with the Doomsdayman might have been audible to the enemy, though that had taken place a thousand feet above the general grouping of friendly forces and more than three thousand feet above the nearest suspected enemy positions.

Finally Jolle spoke—or rather whispered, "Take a break, Captain. I can record any messages incoming." The fourth occupant of the room could be heard standing and walking past the curtain. Then Jolle spoke to Cor and Svir. "We're set. Things are going to rip apart in fifteen minutes unless he anticipates me. I may not have another chance to talk with you before tomorrow—and I want to get this over with before we arrive at O'rmouth."

A cornered animal can only act aggressively, and Svir certainly felt cornered. He hissed back, "That's assuming you win the battle tonight, you bastard." Why didn't the monster make his move?

"Hey, watch those sibilants, friend," Jolle answered quietly. "Part of the reason for this pause is that both sides are making a sound recon. I don't want to get bombed out of my own command post. No. Don't start screaming until I finish my story. OK?"

Svir felt Cor tense beside him. Apparently she had had the same thought. He closed his mouth, and wondered whether Jolle had seen him preparing to shout or had just concluded that that was what he might do. He might as well forget that idea. Jolle could probably kill him before he could yell.

Jolle continued. "There is no chance that we will lose this engagement. We have the high ground, we have the art'ry, and we have some acclimated troops. But this is not the final showdown that our forces think it is. Unless we are lucky, the one called Profirio will survive. This battle is merely an intermediate step, and tomorrow, after our victory, we must move on to the next stage. That is where I need you."

Cor's whisper came faintly. "I'll bet it pleases you to pull off the wings of batlets, too. Why don't you finish? We know you—slaver!"

"You two have jumped to some easy but false conclusions. Have you ever considered that I might have brought you here to kick some sense into your heads? If I wanted to kill you slowly I could do that at my leisure after this affair is over." He didn't wait for a reply to this. "This is really my fault, I suppose. I should have picked you up right after you went through my wagon. Yes, I knew you were the burglar. But we were very busy, and I hadn't counted on Marget reacting as violently as she did to your revelation. You'll have to forgive her; she's—uh—a little unbalanced right now, I think. Even I didn't realize how strongly she's fallen for me.

"But that's passed. I want you back on my side and I have only minutes. What do you think you saw in my wagon this afternoon, Svir?"

They weren't to be killed! At least not yet. Svir sat up. The movement brought a momentary darkness to his mind. "Well, I saw a golem, and it talked with a human voice. So Profirio must be the policeman and you the monster."

The alien sighed. "If only your technology were fifty years more advanced. If only you had more iron on this world. Svir, what you saw was a machine, not too much better than even your people make nowadays. It can think only in the most primitive ways. It displayed abilities that made it seem alive to you—but actually it performed only a few simple tricks. If that box had really been even a moderately smart thinking machine, do you think it would have let you into the wagon? And consider the means it used to lock and unlock the wagon doors. That was a simple—uh—damn, you have no word for it. Call it an optional magnet. If you knew anything about"—again he seemed to search for words—"current changes, you would see the trick was elementary. Someday I'm going to find out how you people have such a good theory of chemistry without knowing about . . . After all you have the valence concept.

"And as for the voice you heard calling for my help, that was as mindless as the trip alarms you have in your homes. They make a screaming wail without words. My little box has an alarm that is just a group of words that are repeated endlessly and without consciousness. Look, you already have machines that can record pictures. Why not sound?"

Tiny doubts had been sown by this speech When he thought back on it, Svir realized that the "golem" had shown no adaptive behavior. If the creature had had any brains, it would have done more to keep him out of the wagon. Perhaps he had only tripped some alarm system after all. Now he saw why the alien had insisted on using magic to explain his science. What would sophisticated machines be like if this sentry device were considered primitive? But he was far from convinced. Perhaps both Profirio *and* Jolle were devils and this was all some bright little game where none of the gods was killed and the locals provided blood. Everything could be a lie. His mind grasped wildly for some working assumption. The only one he had was to believe the original story as Jolle had told it—with the single proviso that Jolle might be the slaver and Profirio the policeman. Until he and Cor could make some decision as to whether Jolle or Profirio was the slaver, they could appear to cooperate with the alien.

He was just opening his mouth when Cor asked, "I think you have us convinced that we can't be convinced of anything. What is the cooperation you want?"

"I guess that is all I could hope for. As to your cooperation, I—Listen." Across the silence of the night came faint but unnaturally clear sounds of voices, occasional screams. The sound of plastic on plastic sounded bell-like in the distance. The sounds were so precise and yet so faint. They reminded Svir of a miniature painting seen under a glass—small and yet filled with complicated details.

The curtain behind them moved, and someone entered the room. "Sir, we have action at Backtrack Five. We believe more enemy troops are moving into that area."

"Very well, Stark, you have my permission to initiate Olive Bat. And send the signal officer in here."

"Right." As the chief of staff left for the map room, Svir struggled to his feet. He blacked out, then came to, clutching at Cor's shoulders for support. Perhaps he wasn't in such good shape as it had seemed when he was sitting. Cor helped him to the dirt-packed wall, and he looked out the window slits. On the other side of his wife he could hear the signalman taking his position. The fibrous bags felt filthy and damp, but leaning against them was safer than trying to balance on his own trembling legs.

The window slits were cunningly constructed to protect against a wide range of art'ry bursts and still allow good overall visibility. Except for the scattering of stars in the narrow strip of visible sky, there was no light.

"There's nothing to see yet," commented Jolle. "This encounter is nearly three miles away and two thousand feet below our horizon."

Svir noticed the flickering light of first one signaler and then another. "The third, fourth, and seventh art'ry batteries acknowledge our command," said the signalman.

Jolle spoke to Svir and Cor. "See, that first flicker was the command from this post. We can't afford to give away our position—in case Pröfe has a suicide squad or a couple of art'ry pieces—so we use runners to take messages from the map room to our signaler. That's about a hundred yards down the hill from here. Then the command is flashed to our units."

The explanation had been purely for their own edification, Svir realized. He wondered what Jolle wanted from him that would be worth such flattering treatment during an important battle.

Then came the *crump* of a single art'ry piece firing below them. The seconds passed, and suddenly there was green daylight over the valley. Back in Bayfast Svir had seen art'ry flares fired over the inland cliffs during maneuvers, and this was much the same. The light moved slowly, dimming and then glowing brightly. But this was not Bayfast. Here the mountains extended thousands of feet above the top of the flare's arc. The unworldly green light illuminated the sides of the gorgelike valley, and in a distortion of perspective the light seemed a tiny green match flickering in a darkened room, casting animated shadows upon the walls and floor. It was nearly as bright as quarter-phase Seraph, and he wasted several seconds watching the shadows shift slowly as the flare drifted across the sky. But even the flare couldn't reveal the extent of the mountains that shouldered over it. To those hulks it was indeed a tiny match flame. As the light dimmed for the last time, Svir pulled his attention down to the ground below them. The terraced fields stretched down a slope of nearly forty-five degrees for a distance of some two thousand feet. Beyond that he could see the road they had come up on from the Picchiu River. The highway stretched transversely across the face of the slope. Beyond that road the ground dipped out of sight. Except for the flare moving across the sky and the sounds of battle from below, there was no sign of human activity.

The flare dimmed, winked out. All was dark again. Svir couldn't even see the stars any more. Then out of the darkness three or four signal lamps flicked on and off as the Crown's observators reported the enemy positions they had sighted. He judged that most of the signalers were near the edge of the drop-off. In the bunker the signal officer was scratching away, taking down all three messages. He spoke to Jolle. "Sir, they say—"

"Never mind, Captain. Just take it into the map room. The men who are going to use this information already have it." As he spoke, the men he referred to took action. In a space of fifteen seconds, the art'ry pieces of the combined Crown and Provincial forces fired. The gunmen had had all their pieces loaded, and they had reacted to the firing instructions instantly. It was no longer necessary to whisper. Though the firing was a couple of thousand feet away, the racket was loud enough to cover most other noises. As the barrage continued, Svir noticed pale lights flickering in the darkness below their position. Even with flashless powder, the guns emitted a pearly, oval radiance when they were fired. It was invisible from below the guns' defilade positions, but the command bunker was in line of sight with most of the guns. They must be well-camouflaged, he thought; when the flare had shone, he had looked at the road and had seen no sign of the guns. Yet the pieces must be within a few feet of the highway: the ground was much too rough to move them further.

A second flare went up. This time there was more to see. At the lip of the steep drop-off that limited their vision, several hundred Rebels had made close contact with friendly forces. It was impossible for Svir to tell whether the loyal forces were Provincial, Crown, or Celestial Servants. Even after the barrage, the noise of their fighting was loud—they were within fifteen hundred feet of the command post itself, though still considerably below it. He realized that even with the flares, the art'ry wasn't very effective. The flares had pinpointed the enemy, but only after they were virtually inside the range of the guns. In daylight the enemy could have been destroyed while still several miles away, but now the friendly troops had to fight just to protect their guns.

And that defense was not entirely successful. Simultaneously with an ear-popping concussion, the crude floor of the bunker bounced up four inches and a minor avalanche of dirt sifted down through the timbered roof. At the same time a finer dust rose from the dirt-packed bags at the front of the room. Svir and Cor held each other for balance, coughed in the smoke-like dust. Ancho cringed at Cor's feet. As the floor steadied, she bent down and picked him up, trying to brush the dust from his coat. Svir could feel the heavy dirt in his hair and down his neck, but the fine dirt seemed to stick to his skin everywhere.

"Damn," spoke Jolle. "They've captured one of our own guns. He's moving much faster than I expected. Unless—" In the green flarelight, Svir saw him pick up a pair of binoculars and inspect the terrain before them. He didn't look at the fighting men moving toward them, but concentrated on the lip of the drop-off, further away. The flare burned out, but he kept watching. The FAO's lights flickered back to the art'ry and command positions.

"Captain," said Jolle, "the enemy has broken our art'ry direction code. The following FAO positions"—he rattled off some map coordinates—"are enemy men pretending to be ours." He paused and watched the messages flickering up from below. "They are directing shells on our own men. Have those positions bombed."

"Yes sir." The signalman started for the curtain. "We'll throw an acknowledge test at them just to make sure."

"You'll destroy them immediately, mister."

"But sir, if they have the main code, how can you tell who the impostors are? And you're just estimating their position. You at least need a—"

Jolle's voice seemed quiet next to the art'ry fire below, but it cut through all the random noises with a cool deadliness. "Captain, I gave you an order. Obey it, or join the enemy."

For a moment the captain struggled to find his voice. "Y-yessir. They'll be destroyed immyest." He disappeared.

"That was a clever move," continued Jolle, "though I'm sure Profirio knew that it would be obvious to me. But then, what he really wants is confusion, so he can escape from his own forces—which are sure to lose—and insinuate himself into the Doomsday group." Svir wondered why the alien troubled to explain these intrigues to him, a mere playing piece. Did Jolle really think this apparent frankness would convince him of his sincerity?

Some of the enemy forces had cleared the drop-off and were still advancing, so that now the art'ry shells were landing on the terrace areas that were in the line of sight of the bunker. The bursts were much more impressive than by day. Red, orange, and even some blue glimmered in the bursting shells—and there seemed to be a fiery structure inside the explosion. The shrap bombs were comparatively less impressive, but from the screams and general turmoil, Svir guessed they were doing more damage. A third flare arced across the valley. Several thousand more enemy soldiers had passed the road. They were close! Somehow they had gutted their way over the lip of the drop-off. But the picture of a horde advancing unstoppably was an illusion that vanished even as the flare dimmed out. They were a large group of men. But they were advancing toward an undefined goal—unless they knew the position of the command post—and they were not in close contact with the friendlies. In short, their mass was gun fodder. The gunmen didn't need any directions to bring their fire directly in on the enemy troops, though some of the nearer guns were too close to the enemy to be effective. The enemy was so close now that the shells lit the battlefield with a stop-action glare that reduced the scene of writhing turmoil to a series of flashing still pictures done in red and orange. Each could have stood on its own as a surrealist representation of pain and death—if anyone had had the skill and the sadism to preserve it.

And only two men knew what the soldiers were dying for—knew whether they were dying to save or to destroy a world.

"Move!" Over the shrieking combination of human pain and exploding bombs, Jolle's voice came by his ear. At the same moment the dirt-packed bag in front of his face exploded in a shower of dirt. It had probably been a quarrel from a heavy crossbow.

The horde that was now a mob moved past them and the art'ry fire followed. Now the noise was muted, coming through the dirt around them. The bomb bursts still cast light across the fields, but they were not directly visible. Svir could now hear a strange sound he hadn't noticed before. It was a snapping, popping sound, like a machine clattering. The sounds came from the left, to the side of the assault they had just observed. He leaned to the right and tried to see around that corner of the slit. A white flashing, something like a signaler, could be seen flickering on and off, much faster than most signalers and without the dots, dashes, and intermeds which characterize a signaling pattern. Jolle gazed into the darkness at the white flicker. "He's bringing on his secret weapon," he said, "but it won't help him."

"Yes, but what is it?" To Svir the flashing light seemed innocuous.

"It's, uh, a hand-held gun. I knew that Pröfe had looted the warehouses in Kotta-svo-Picchiu. He probably got something like two thousand ounces of iron there. He apparently used some of it to make a repeating gun, small enough to be carried. I don't think he's actually built a nonmetallic hand gun—I tried that, but couldn't do it. He has at least five men down there with—" He stopped as orange blossoms of fire burst over the twinkling lights, outshining them. When the fire cores faded, the white sparklings were gone too.

The battle sounds were sporadic now. Guns still fired and men still fought, but it was the tempo of grease sputtering in a pan rather than of a fire burning before a strong wind. Was the battle over?

"See that." Jolle pointed to one of the signal lights. "We've destroyed virtually all of the enemy's main force." He laughed. "This is almost perfect. The engagement lasted only thirty minutes, and we've achieved complete victory. We'll probably be able to capture most of the survivors. Things moved so fast, we may have actually caught

Pröfe in the massacre." He turned to the signalman who had just returned. "Captain, go back to the map room and find out if any enemy units made it past us."

Svir looked at Jolle. The fighting had set fire to the fields, and burning grain faintly illuminated the alien's face. He appeared to be smiling, but his face was glistening with sweat. What if the engagement had destroyed Profirio? Then the whole matter was decided, since Svir could do nothing on his own to destroy Jolle, and there was no possibility that he could persuade Tatja to oppose the alien.

"I'll have to leave you in a few minutes," said Jolle. "I want to supervise the inspection of prisoners. Marget handled that during the battle, but I think she would have a lot of trouble if Pröfe were captured. But before I go, let me tell you what I want from you. Tomorrow morning the command group is going to O'rmouth. The Doomsday people think this is all some sort of victory celebration, and we won't dispel that notion until we're in conference with the Archobservers. I don't think I've convinced you that Pröfe is the monster, but I need you, and if you have any questions or tests to put to me, think them over tonight and maybe I can give you some proof before we go up there. When we're actually in conference, I want—"

He stopped, brought his attention back to the terrain outside. Svir followed his gaze. Some thirty yards to the right of front was one of the few trees that grew in the area. Its stunted, twisted limbs had given it a horrible manlike appearance during the artillery bombardment. Now, in the light of the fires around the bomb craters, it looked like a monster crippled by the fighting—though compared with the real horrors outside, this effect was diminished. What was Jolle upset about? All about were the sounds of mop-up squads and wounded and dying men, but nothing else. What would Profirio do if he discovered the command post? That tree was near enough so that if the alien were hiding behind it, he could throw a bomb through the slit windows of the bunker and in an instant change his virtual defeat to total victory. Svir licked his lips nervously, tasting sweat and dust. Cor must have been thinking along the same lines, for she moved closer to him, grabbing his arm for support. He hugged her briefly and reached up to pet Ancho, who was stirring nervously on her shoulder.

Then the tree spoke. It was a human voice: ponderous, deep, and menacing. The words weren't Spräk or Sfierro. To his Island mind they sounded something like, "*Ter äshe gaul,* Jolle." And he never forgot those words, for simultaneously two other events occurred which bent his life out of time.

Jolle's viselike hand jerked Svir back from the slit window. "Prö—" he began.

Then the world turned red. It was as if the earth had been ripped apart and, through the narrow crack produced, the light of hell itself burned. With the beam of bloody light came a painfully loud explosion just inches before his face. Then the rent was mended. He was lying on the ground, and everything was dark except for the painful blue afterimages floating in his eyes. He felt Cor beside him. Jolle was pulling him into a crouching position. He allowed himself to be raised, then reached for his wife. "C'mon Cor, get up." No answer. Then he was back on the ground, feeling for wounds . . . trying to wake her . . . burning fur . . . Ancho . . .

That stroke of artificial lightning had come through the slit near his left side—where Cor had been standing. And the explosion had been . . . He still couldn't see anything, but he could hear someone screaming her name over and over. Strong hands pulled him up and someone was slapping his face. The tiny room was filled with people. Or rather he had been moved into the map room. The streak afterimage of Pröfe's weapon still hung before his eyes, but now there was another, fainter light. He was lying on his back, and the room's algae pot was shining above him like a broad blue cloud. It seemed so much fainter than before. Everything was dark and blurred.

He rolled over in the dirt. Tall forms stood over something on the ground. Other things, people, ran back and forth, but they were irrelevant. The kneeling one was a medic, he could see now. And beside him on the ground—his sight was, luckily, very blurred, and the impression was vague, but—The explosion at the end of the red thunder bolt had been—Cor's face.

The tired medic muttered something. "It was quick at least." The platitude sent Svir into a flat dive that ended at the medic's throat. He was on top of him, then under, and the noise around him seemed bright with surprise and anger. Then everything became dark again.

CHAPTER 17

Recorded history began on the island chains of Tu. There were stories that the race had been born on The Continent, but they were only legends. The colonization of The Continent had begun more than a thousand years before. The western coast of The Continent had been colonized by two different cultures. The first was from the Llerenito islands. Their agricultural colonies stretched from the equator to the fortieth parallel. Later the Islanders of the Chainpearl, Tsanart, and Osterlai Archipelagates planted the first colonies in the area of Bayfast. At virtually the same time, a smaller group from the Osterlais set up precarious fishing communities north of the fortieth parallel. This group had originally spoken the same language and had had the same cultural heritage as their cousins much further to the south around Bayfast. In fact, many of the names they gave their lands were recognizable—the word Doomsday for instance. But the years passed, and the distance and hardships became too great to maintain a cultural allegiance to the Islands or to the far South. The population moved inland after the discovery of metals in the Doomsday peaks.

After five hundred years, though they still spoke a language understandable to the Bayfastlings, their world view was far more different from that of Bayfast than were the once-strange cultures of Picchiu and Sfierranyi Provinces. These last had originally been immersed in the Llerenito milieu, with its totemic religion and triple standard. But as they came under the political and economic domination of Crownesse, they had gradually lost their peculiar customs. And now, except for language differences, their inhabitants were indistinguishable from Bayfastlings.

The people who eventually called themselves Doomsdaymen founded a new religion—which probably would have become Seraph worship if only the Doomsday mountain had been beneath the same sky that held Seraph. In the beginning the Doomsday religion had been a complex astrological cult whose central belief was that the sky of night was the physical manifestation of the most powerful spirit, and that by studying its countenance, all problems could be solved. In the hills near the modern city of Kotta-svo-Picchiu there were ruins of the complex astrological temples and ramps that the first Observers had constructed.

Perhaps the Doomsday religion would have remained a crackpot cult dominating a minor fishing people if two other elements had not entered the picture. The first was the development of lenses. This invention seemed to both priests and fishermen evidence of divinely inspired progress in understanding the ways of God, and brought the Doomsday cult total political control over the lay people of the villages. The second development, some two hundred years after the introduction of the telescope, was the discovery of copper and iron in the Doomsday mountains. In one century the fishermen became miners, and very rich ones. Their culture changed from a poor but self-sufficient one to an extremely wealthy one totally dependent on foreign trade.

The villages along the coast disappeared, except for Kotta-svo-Picchiu, which ballooned into a large port. At the same time, scores of small, busy, primitive mining villages grew in the highlands, and some became cities. The high priests—or Archobservers—of the Doomsday cult found themselves the absolute rulers of one of the wealthiest and most inaccessible countries in the world. Now they had the resources to search the face of God as befitted that sacred undertaking. As the search for iron carried the ex-fishermen higher into the mountains, the priests noticed that the nights were clearer, the stars brighter.

Thus was born the concept of a cathedral at the top of the world. They would find the highest point in the

Doomsday mountains and construct there the largest telescope possible. The priests counted on the job taking more than a century and all the resources of the people of Doomsday. But if the priests had realized how difficult their undertaking would prove to be, perhaps even they would have quailed. It took them nearly fifty years to reach a point ten thousand feet below the peak they judged to be the highest in the world, and another twenty-five years to construct a road that would reach that intermediate point. The first explorers had named that point Overmouth, since it stood above the wide mouth of the largest glacier in the range. In the years that followed, the priests nearly gave up the idea of proceeding higher. It was an immense task simply to create a large settlement at O'rmouth. Perhaps the heights above were reserved for intermediate gods, and mere humans should construct their observatory at O'rmouth. For even at that altitude the unacclimated lived less than thirty months, and children often died before they reached the age of two months.

It was only in the last seventy years that this terrible thinness in the air had been conquered and a means of reaching the top of the world discovered. By then O'rmouth had a population of nearly thirty thousand and rich ore deposits had been found in the area, so that the city was both the political and the economic capital of the area. The drive to the top of the world could be undertaken. It only cost sixty years, and fifteen thousand lives, to set the sixty-inch Eye in its shrine.

"So? We are grateful. We are so grateful that we will not ask of Your Most Sacred Majesty reparations for the damage her armies have done to the Riverside Road, to Kotta-svo-Picchiu, to the Kotta Eye, and to our farmlands below O'rmouth." Mikach the Perceptive, First Arch-observer, spoke with unconcealed sarcasm, but with all the dignity of his station. He wore the powder blue robes which indicated that he spoke as a temporal power. A composition of diamonds, rubies, and emeralds, set in a copper necklace, cascaded down the blouse of his robe. The white hair of his face and head was braided into two thick tails, one going down his back, the other down his front. On his head was the yard-high cone of one point, his "crown." Beside him at the broad iron-topped table sat other Archobservers. Behind them stood unbearded Observers, wearing the shorter, pyramidal caps of their office.

"Yes, and for our part, we are grateful for the services of your Servants in defeating the Insurrectionists." Tatja spoke quickly but without apparent effort. While the priests wore ornaments of jewels, her basic dress was of a material that seemed to be constructed of thousands of tiny gems, each glittering with its own color. Over this were strewn larger gems and curved plates of the principal metals. Feathery spider silk floated about the ensemble, first concealing and then revealing different facets of the dress. Her shining red hair flowed smoothly from beneath the silver and gold Crown—the second Crown of all the Crowns.

Around her sat the highest advisors to the Crown. First on the right was Jolle, still in the uniform of a Provincial Militia general. Though in combat that uniform had seemed a foppery, it was really quite plain compared to the incandescent costumes around it. Behind them sat military commanders and cabinet officers. No Picchiui or Crown's Man was standing—at these altitudes, it took some effort just to walk. Except for the Doomsdaymen, the only people who seemed at ease were Jolle and Tatja. All the others were in a constant struggle with the dizziness and nausea that even the faintest exertion brought. Just minutes before, Imar Stark had been carried from the conference with bloody vomit on his lips.

Tatja continued, "But we do believe that your debt to us is greater than ours to you. We have only a small request of you as our vassals. You grant me—or at least claim to grant to me—the ultimate temporal sovereignty over your lands. I wish to visit the High Eye, and to perform there a simple experiment."

Mikach the Perceptive stiffened, and among the observers behind them there was murmuring. When the Doomsdayman spoke, it was with deep and frank indignation. "Marget, you know us well—well enough to know that your request is entirely beyond the bounds of our hospitality. Only those who are trained *and* faithful may approach that sacred instrument. You are in our capital city because of your—titular—sovereignty over us. If you insist, we will permit you the use of the ten-inch ceremonial instrument here at O'rmouth—and you must know what a concession this is. But if you continue to blaspheme thus, you will be cast down from our heights—by my temporal power."

As he spoke, Tatja glanced at Jolle, who shook his head slightly. The others in the party came full alert at this threat of physical violence, reached for the crossbows and daggers that they did not have. The Doomsdaymen in the chamber were unarmed also, as a gesture of fealty. Several of the Crown's generals came halfway to their feet. Only the Astronomer Royal seemed unaffected by the threat. In fact, he was not listening. His gaze moved idly from one object to the next in the low room. To the right, the high glass windows gave a wide, clear view of O'rmouth and the glacier below. Svir's gaze flickered away. He looked without interest at the stony city spread before the windows. Though the city was protected from avalanches by the arrangement of the slopes above, there were still minor slides and extremely heavy snows during the Waterfall. Thus every building, even the lowliest residential cooperative, was built of stone blocks. It was difficult to imagine how even acclimated individuals could have constructed those buildings. There were rumors that the Doomsdaymen had domesticated the half-intelligent mountain apes and used them for such work.

The granite walls were decorated with carved gargoyles, and the corners of the more important buildings were studded with dovetailed stone cylinders. In some ways the Doomsdaymen had no imagination. They kept the architectural forms that they had originally used for building wooden cabins on the coast. Now the false-log effect was taken as a sign of ancient nobility.

The roofs of the buildings below were covered with several feet of snow, even this late in the season, though the narrow streets were cleared. The roofs had low gables. In fact, most appeared flat. During Waterfall, the snow covered everything. Thus most buildings were of two stories, the second much broader and overhanging the first. But if the design was not beautiful, it was well thought out. The roofs of the buildings on the opposite sides of a street were only three or four feet apart, so the snow quickly filled the gap and then formed an arch across the street. During the snows the city streets were tunnels.

In the streets below, children ran and played, unaware that such exertions were impossible to any but them. The Doomsdaymen believed in large families. Mortality was high at all ages and there was chronic underemployment. One day soon those children would find that arduous labor was the fate of all but a few Doomsdaymen, and they would wear the dull gray and brown uniforms of adult commoners.

The entire city was crammed into two hundred acres to take advantage of the avalanche shade. Nowhere in that low mass of carved stone and dirty snow was a bit of green visible.

Beyond the town the scene was magnificent. They were far above the lands of the world, and the view was like looking down from heaven. The sharp white points of mountain peaks poked up from below, and thousands of feet below them, the raw stone showed gray and brown and yellow. Still farther down, but in crystal detail through the clear air, the uppermost farmlands and the timberlines could be seen. Below that was the glacier's mouth. The glacier wound for miles between the peaks of the range, a frozen river with dozens of tributaries. Brown flow lines were clearly visible where the millions of tons of rock had been gouged from the mountains. The mouth of the glacier, where the ice melted, became the head waters of the Picchiu River. But this was hidden from view by the shoulder of the slope on which the city rested.

Cor. For an instant that dragged by eternally, the screaming in the back of his mind broke through the passive numbness that separated thought from reality. Cor with the smooth black hair. Cor with the brown eyes, the creamy skin, the soft, firm, full body. Cor with the strength to support him through all problems, to work in so many ways to make his days bright. Cor with the face that—The charred horror of last night's vision blasted him out of that line of thought.

It was still impossible to believe that she had gone away and would never be back. In a way, life seemed like a supple tree limb that grew smoothly in an anticipated direction. Then Coronadas Ascuasenya, in a single burning moment, was ripped from the universe, and the smooth young branch was snapped across. Reddish sap flowed out, leaving the end dead. Reality took a new, unrecognized turn, leaving the branch bruised, torn. It would be weeks before the new reality seemed substantial and inescapable. Until that full realization came, it was possible to retreat into the world that was not and to imagine for short periods that things were otherwise—or at least to forget what things had become.

And so Jolle's quiet words to him that morning, as he pleaded for some undefined help during this meeting, had gone uncomprehended. The pleas were from a nightmare, perhaps-not world, and he could ignore them. But as time passed, the screaming at the back of his mind broke through more often and he knew that eventually he would be pushed irretrievably into the new reality. Then apathy would become hate, and he would move blindly and probably ineffectively to destroy the creature who had destroyed the only girl foolish enough to love Svir Hedrigs. Profirio had fooled many people, but he had here an enemy whose hate could overwhelm any persuasion. This last thought brought him closer to the new reality than at any time in the last twelve hours. His friends, after all, were making plans that would result in the destruction of Profirio.

Tatja, using her most imperial manner, was still working at Mikach. "Very well, Archobserver, if we may not visit the Eye in our persons, I would like you to conduct an experiment there at our direction."

The Perceptive One didn't answer at once. Perhaps this approach might work. "What is the experiment?"

"A limited sky search."

"How limited?"

"Depending on how accurate our information is, it could take from one to twenty hours of observation time."

As a matter of fact, it could take as long as three hundred hours if Jolle's intuition were in error by even a small amount.

"And what do you expect to find?"

In this case the truth was the perfect answer. Tatja smiled as she said, "My astronomer believes that the Tu-Seraph system has an external satellite."

"Ridiculous. You've seen our reports in the past. Don't you read them? There is no satellite more than ten yards across nearer than one million miles. I certainly won't allow such redundant use of the High Eye. We have done some experiments for you in the past because they were interesting. But in this request, you go too far."

The Queen sat straight in her portable throne, touched her crown, and spoke flatly to Mikach. This was the last verbal weapon she had. "Subject, I demand your cooperation. Am I not sovereign?"

The other's voice was just as grim. There was no hint of sarcasm, but the tone was unyielding and deadly. "You are sovereign as long as you remain in Bayfast and mind your own affairs. But here you are out of your element. Here your forces may outnumber ours, but each of us is worth five of you in open combat, as you no doubt discovered last night. If you give up these demands, we will allow you to depart in peace, friendship, and lealty, for we realize that you have the power to control Kotta-svo-Picchiu and the Riverside Road, and to choke our commerce. But if you persist in this imperialist heresy, we will destroy you." He half-rose from his seat, then sat down abruptly. Standing in another's presence was regarded as a form of self-subordination. As an Orthodox cultist, his beliefs were more closely related to simple astrology than some of the Reformist Observers, who were more interested in straight scientific research than temporal power. The Reformists might have been more susceptible to Marget's request, but unfortunately they were out of power in this decade.

"If that is your final answer, Mikach, then I am sorry. I won't try to dignify what we're going to do by calling you a disloyal subject. The overlord ploy was a stunt. I know I can't control you people—at least not for indefinite periods. And we need your metals. So after this is over, please remember that we will always be ready to resume commerce with you."

The Archobserver's anger dissipated before this nebulous attack. He obviously had no idea what was coming.

"Last night you saw the effects of one of our weapons—artillery. I believe you call them bomb throwers." Several men in Doomsday blue caught the drift, and their eyes widened. But apparently Mikach was not so perceptive.

He replied, "Yes, they are catapults, aren't they?"

"More than that, Mikach. What you saw last night was a very limited demonstration. We were operating at the minimum range possible—about six thousand feet. We can project bombs more than five miles horizontally with these weapons. And the maximum vertical range is more than—"

Mikach interrupted with an inarticulate roar. He was on his feet in an instant, and he took a swing at Tatja's throat. "You'll die for this, infidel! To think we aided you last night because you ascribed your own treachery to your enemy." The priest turned to signal the doorman. Outside the conference room stood the Crown's personal guard and a squad of Celestial Servants. If Mikach gave the word, there would be a massacre.

"Sit down, Mikach," Jolle said. His voice was not remarkably loud, nor even tense, but the Archobserver turned back to face the Crown.

Tatja took advantage of this moment of dampened fury. "We aren't foolish, Mikach. If we don't return, or if you hold me and my staff for ransom, then the plan goes into effect without any communication from us. So why don't you do as General Jolle says. Sit down and hear the rest." The other sat down. She knew the priest had in that instant signaled the Servants outside to be ready to overpower the Royal Guards. She must speak quickly and convince Mikach of her side's invincibility. "You've guessed what we're going to do. My artillery is under orders to destroy the High Eye at my command, and under certain other circumstances.

"You've seen how destructive even a single high-explosive shell is. Don't doubt the accuracy of our fire. Though the guns are fourteen thousand feet below the target, I assure you that my gunmen can place one out of two shells within one hundred feet of the mirror. In fact, the location of your mirror is one of the most exactly measured points in the world, and the best mapmakers use your coordinates as a base point. I suggest that you do not attack the artillery pieces. They are vulnerable, but there are nearly two hundred of them. *At this moment* they are loaded and aimed. You could not destroy them all before they put out your Eye.

"Under this duress, we again ask you to permit a party of my people to ascend to the Eye, and to conduct an experiment. We will not harm the instrument. Repara—"

"No! Better to destroy it cleanly than by taint." The priest's pasty white face had become momentarily flushed and puffy. Behind him there was a barely perceptible exchange of glances between Reformist Observers. They preferred taint to destruction.

It was Jolle who answered the dogmatism. "You blaspheme, Mikach. The face of God will still stand billions of light-years beyond your blue, whether your Eye is put out or spat upon. Spittle may be expunged, but if your Eye be destroyed, then you will be lost from the inner mysteries of God."

It was a Reformist argument couched in Orthodox jargon. For a moment Mikach was silent. He realized that most of his supporters were thinking the thoughts just voiced by the black-bearded fellow wearing the militia uniform. The priest's face was pale again, and only the trembling of his voice and lips betrayed the struggle within him. He neither nodded nor explicitly stated his submission, but asked, "When will you ascend, then?"

Tatja answered, "Sometime in the afternoon. Say twenty-six hours. We'll stay here and rest until then."

Now the other nodded. "Very well. We'll clear some quarters for you." He leaned across the table, and for a moment his face twisted with the anger demonstrated moments before. "My people will dedicate much of their remaining existence to punishing you for this."

The generals behind Tatja smiled at this threat made by

the leader of a second-rate military power against the most powerful nation in the world. Tatja didn't laugh. If she had been nothing more than the Queen of Crownesse, this would have been a threat to fear. She respected the determination and technical intelligence that lay behind all the outward irrationality of the Doomsdayman. Mikach's promise was the sort which starts crusades.

CHAPTER 18

Someone had given him a crossbow. It was a durable model, its cross-spars angled back. On one full winding it could fire all six bolts in its magazine. And each bolt was filled with enough explosive powder to put a hole through three inches of wood.

At the moment Svir felt no curiosity as to why he, who barely knew how to sight a bow, had been given the weapon. He had not noticed that out of the two-hundred-man party, only Jolle, Tatja, and he were armed.

Jolle and Tatja had originally planned to make the ascent alone, but the ingenious Doomsdaymen had made that impossible. The priests claimed that all the picturemaking equipment had just ten days before been brought down to O'rmouth for a general overhaul. This was plausible, since the observatory itself was not large enough to contain a complete machine shop. Unfortunately, more than a hundred bearers were then needed to carry the picturemaking equipment necessary to Jolle's project. The Doomsdaymen used a much more cumbersome picturemaking technique than the greentint method developed in the islands; but their technique had several important advantages for astronomical applications, and this made up for the massive equipment necessary. There also had to be a number of Crown's Men along to watch the mob of potential saboteurs. Virtually everyone was surprised that these troops were to go unarmed. The Doomsdaymen were pleased with the situation, and the Crown's Men were frankly angry.

If he had thought about it, Svir would have understood why only the three of them were armed, but he still wandered in a daydream. His mind was absorbed in the rhythmic task of walking up the steep tunnel toward the top of the world. The tunnel was just below the level where the pack snow became fluffy and blew before the wind that swept across the face of the mountain at more than forty miles per hour. Except during the Turnabout, those winds were a constant blast. Even here, safely below the open air, the wind produced a flutish hum through the length of the tunnel. And when they walked beneath the ventilation holes that were stuck through the roof of the tunnel every forty feet or so, the hum became a scream. The bright afternoon sunlight that must make the snowfields above glow burning white cast circles of light on the floor of the tunnel and illuminated the figures moving slowly up the incline.

In several areas the tunnel was so steep that it had steps cut in the ice of its floor to form staircases which sometimes extended for a thousand feet. Yet this journey was a walk in paradise compared to the climb that had faced the first explorers. Then it had been necessary to climb across the top of the snow, through the wind. And though the slope was really quite slight compared to the upper approaches to most peaks, the atmospheric pressure at the top was only one-fifth the pressure at sea level. It was difficult to maintain body temperature, much less work in that air. If it had not been for what the Doomsdaymen called the "perfume of life," no amount of fanaticism and wealth would have made the construction of the High Eye possible.

The perfume of life—to the "heathen" Island chemists, this was simply oxygen. At sea level the partial pressure of oxygen is something like three pounds per square inch. At O'rmouth it was 1.4 psi. And as had been known for more than a century, it was the partial pressure of oxygen that determined whether the air could sustain life—thus oxygen was the perfume of life. For the last forty years the Doomsdaymen had used the technique of differential liquefaction to produce large amounts of oxygen. The oxygen was compressed into containers and allowed to escape slowly—as perfume might from an aerator. With some skill, it was possible to raise the partial oxygen pressure at the observatory from 0.6 psi to 1.4 psi, even though the total pressure inside the observatory was the same as the pressure outside. It was simple and effective.

No hermetic seals were necessary.

Thirty men pulled the carts carrying the spun-glass oxygen tanks. The scentless perfume could occasionally be heard behind the hum of the wind. For the benefit of the Crown's Men, Tatja had insisted on bringing enough tanks to maintain a partial pressure of 2.0 psi. Thus, though the air was thinner than even at O'rmouth, the Crown's men were more comfortable than they had been since they passed the twelve thousand-foot level.

They had been in march for nearly seven hours. Even with the relatively rich air, Svir was a single ache from his waist down. With each step, bright spurts of pain surged up his calves and the middle of his gut responded with a sympathetic throb. Where before, the simple task of walking had made it easy for him to retreat from the events around him, now each step forced him to be aware

Wiping sweat from his eyes, he looked up to examine the party. The Doomsdaymen were as fatigued as the Crown's Men. It was a Doomsday custom that since the night was twenty hours long, man was meant to sleep twenty hours. And since the day was also twenty hours, man was meant to wake and work during that period. Most Doomsdaymen had never seen the brilliance that Seraph could bring to the sky, so they didn't realize how mutable the night could be. Only Observers were exempt from the custom, so most of the Doomsdaymen who accompanied them had been up for the last eighteen hours.

Several times the group had become so spread along the tunnel that the dissipating oxygen could not cover everyone adequately. Then, without any warning, walking became impossible, and Tatja or Jolle had them change formation and redistribute the tanks so that everyone was within ten feet of a "perfume" container.

For the first time in more than twenty hours, Svir found himself fully in contact with the events around him. Cor was dead. He believed that. And now that he believed it, the hate he felt for her murderer could blossom into his consciousness. Profirio must die—not because he wished to destroy a race, but because he had destroyed the most important person in the universe. As a mere human, Svir had no chance of accomplishing this mission, but he had two friends behind him, and he also had a weapon. For the moment then, there was purpose in his hanging around, though with success would return failure.

It was very dark in the tunnel. The Doomsdaymen never used algae pots, and a torch would burn more oxygen than one hundred men. Only an occasional glow came from overhead when the tunnel cut close to the surface or when they passed beneath a ventilation hole. But that direct light was fading now as the sun moved closer to the horizon and its light could no longer shine down the vertical ventilation pipes. Nevertheless, he could occasionally see the other men. Most walked bent before the carts they pulled. He knew that Jolle and Tatja were walking behind the entire group. It was a strategic certainty that one of those men who appeared so tired was actually alert, calculating. By walking behind the rest, the Queen and the alien could watch most of the group with their sensitive eyes, and if they did not discover Profirio, they at least would not be surprised from behind.

Svir ended up near the front of the van. Even if the tunnel were well lighted, his two friends would have been out of sight, since the group was spread along one hundred yards of tunnel, and since the tunnel was not in a straight line.

If he were Profirio, would he not choose a point far forward, just for the reason that he would not be under the others' constant observation?

He looked about with new interest. Who seemed a bit too lively? That was probably the wrong thing to look for: Profirio must be a great actor. Under other circumstances these thoughts would have filled him with fear: it was dark, the figures were indistinct, and one of those men, perhaps right behind him, was a monster more evil than any in the history of the world.

He was abruptly aware that he was cold. He pulled the parka closer to his body.

There was conversation nearby. Low muttering came past the sounds of the wind. There was more than one voice—maybe three or four. Apparently people will grumble and talk even when exhausted. One of those voices could be Profirio's. For wouldn't the alien be gathering supporters? No doubt he was just as fiendishly persuasive as Tatja and Jolle.

Svir dropped back till he was even with the sounds. The tunnel was hardly wider than a single cart, and now he saw that his prospects were right in front of a cart. One of them was pulling it. The six-foot tank on the cart emitted its perfume in a tiny but unending whine.

Then a hand closed on his shoulder. He leaped half a foot into the air, his larynx paralyzed with shock. He spastically squeezed the trigger of the crossbow, but the safety was engaged and he was spared the mortal embarrassment of shooting himself with an explosive bolt.

"Sorry, friend, I slipped."

Svir turned to look at the other. It was possible that the fellow *had* slipped. Even though the floor of the tunnel was covered with decomposed granite, there were open patches of ice. But at the head of the van, these patches were without the slippery film of water that developed after fifty or sixty people had passed across them. The man released his arm. There was a momentary glimmer from above, and Svir saw that he was fairly old, though muscular.

This could be it! It seemed to Svir that the other's face showed just a bit too much fatigue. What was more, the man was a Celestial Servant—one of the Doomsday soldiers. If Profirio had indeed insinuated himself into the party, he probably was posing as a Servant, since the Crown's Men had been carefully chosen for this journey.

Svir made no attempt to start a conversation. He had a dubious advantage over Profirio. The alien must nullify the armed men in the party. Since Svir was one-third of that force, Profirio would either manipulate him with conversation—or kill him. Perhaps the limited number of ploys in this game would for once make it possible for Svir to compete with a mind like Tatja's. When the "old soldier" finally spoke, Svir felt a flash of triumph. Now he knew who to watch when they reached the observatory.

"You're one of the Crown's Men, aren't you?" The soldier's voice seemed a bit too relaxed compared with his panting exhaustion of moments before.

"That's right," Svir replied, with as much disinterest as he could muster.

"I don't mean offense, but I see you're armed. You must be important. Maybe you can tell me. Why are you doing this?"

"Doing what?" His reply was not an evasion. The Servant's question seemed disconnected from the dangers that floated through his mind.

"Why do you trespass here? Why do you insult a religion that's never done you harm?" The voice had an innocent, bewildered tone.

The official reason was that this was Marget's whim. To her cabinet she had presented no more explanation, though most of those officials were happy to humor her. They thought the Doomsdaymen were dangerously arrogant. Certainly Svir couldn't blurt out the real reason for this trip—only Profirio would believe that.

"Perhaps you thought," the Servant continued, since Svir seemed bound to silence, "that we didn't show you proper respect. I love my people, sir, and I love my religion. But I've been south. I know that we're actually a pretty mean group. All we really have beyond a beautiful stretch of wasteland is the conviction that we are especially blessed by the All Powerful. Our leaders must be arrogant. If they weren't, most of them would have no reason to stay here. And if the centuries have bred anything into Doo'd'en, it's that this land must be held at any cost."

Old foot soldiers could be this sharp, but it seemed impossible that any ordinary soldier could express himself so smoothly, and with such a vocabulary. Svir set his thumb on the bow's safety.

The Servant went on, "But for all their arrogance, our leaders helped you—when they were sure that the enemy forces could never reach our level. We make a big show of fierceness, you know. But we really have no time to learn the military arts. This was the first time in two hundred years that Celestial Servants have been in combat. We always thought military drill was a frivolous, enjoyable pastime—because no one ever died, as they so often do in mine and construction work. But this morning my men—"

"Your men?" Svir broke in, trying to keep the right amount of curiosity in his voice.

"Yes, I'm a Celestial Servant with Radiant Effulgence.

That's about the same as a colonel of infantry in your table of organization."

Damn. That could explain his diction.

"It was—strange to see men die, fighting. We thought we were protecting people or land. Now we see we might as well not have fought at all—or even have fought on the other side. What was the point?" The voice was puzzled, bewildered, and Svir for an instant felt the same puzzlement. Perhaps Jolle and Tatja and Profirio were puppets on some higher god's strings, and so on in an ascending sequence. He turned to reply, but the other had dropped further back in the formation. Emotionally Svir was convinced of the fellow's sincerity. In a perverse way, this seemed the most powerful indication that he had been speaking to the illusive Profirio—the ability to convince was one of Tatja's most obvious talents, and the same applied to Jolle. When you were sure they were sincere—then you knew you had been fooled. He brought his crossbow to port arms, turned, and let the oxygen wagon creak past him. The other was gone. At least, none of the vague shapes nearby walked with the "old soldier's" hesitant stumble.

Now he was sure. If he saw the other again, he would chance killing an innocent man. Maybe that was why the other moved away. But then, why hadn't Profirio killed him? The alien certainly could have done that barehanded and without noise.

In a space of less than three hundred feet, the sound of the wind dropped away. Actually, the observatory was not quite at the top of the peak. There was a ridge fifty feet high and several hundred yards from the observatory itself that helped shield the buildings from wind and snow. The tunnel had entered the wind shadow of this ridge. Soon the snow blanket should be too shallow to contain the tunnel. Svir wondered what the Doomsdaymen had done with that problem He nearly tripped on the step up, as the floor changed from ice to stone. Everything was dark. There was no stray light, as in the snow tunnel. As the carts behind him were lifted laboriously over the step, he felt the walls. They were stone brick. If the observatory itself were constructed this way, it must be a pretty dreary place, with no view except of heaven. Too bad. It was still daylight outside, and the view that spread below the highest spot in the world was likely spectacular.

The group moved forward through the darkness. All he could hear were footsteps and the creaking wheels. Then someone brushed past him, moving fast. He lashed out, struck something soft.

"It's me," said Tatja. He realized they were moving quietly to the head of the file so that they would be the first to enter the observatory. Jolle was taking no chances. Svir tried to follow them, but they were virtually running through the darkness.

He wanted to tell them that one of the Servants was Profirio. But they were already too far ahead of him. He had to slow down and cautiously feel his way. Ahead, they had found a door, and someone was pounding on it. It would be an interesting bit of treachery if the High Eye Observers chose not to open that door. The party certainly didn't have enough oxygen to make it back down to O'rmouth.

But the gunners thousands of feet below, where there was still grass and air, had instructions to open fire unless they received certain coded assurances from Tatja at given times. And this point had been made excruciatingly clear to the Doomsdaymen at O'rmouth, who, by a series of heliographs, relayed the threat to the astronomers at the High Eye.

A trapezoid of bright yellow light appeared ahead as the door opened. He squinted at the brilliance. For a moment the interior of the rough stone hall was lit. Beyond that doorway, just a few feet away, was the object of the long journey.

CHAPTER 19

Dazzling sunlight was everywhere. Glass windows filled much of the wall space, and beyond them was the view from the top of the world. The sky was almost indigo, as if the sun had already set, though it was still late afternoon. Spread below that blue hemisphere were the mountains of the Doomsday range. The peaks might have been frozen waves of brilliant white tossed on a frozen sea. Here and there the white masses were fluffy rather than angular: these were clouds hung about some of the peaks. The arrangement was such that the glacier was not visible. But there was a faint band of brown at the horizon, which might have been an illusion caused by the westering sun or which might have been the edge of the still-unexplored Central Desert.

There were places in the near distance where the brown and yellow limestone showed through the powder snow. The western windows gave a clear view of the naked rock that rose some fifty feet to shield the Observatory. Through the nearest windows the yellow exterior of the stone hallway could be seen. Light snow lay powdery in the cracks and joints of the yellow stonework, but further away, where the hallway moved out of the wind shadow, the snow swirled and blew into constantly changing patterns on the hallway. About four hundred feet from the observatory, the hallway became a true tunnel as it sank beneath the permanent snow bank.

Near this point stood a wind turbine with its snout pointed into the wind, its blades whirling. At the base of its derrick was a contraption of gears and pistons. A covered trough extended from the turbine to the observatory. The trough was sheathed by ice, and a thick haze of steam or ice billowed around it. Evidently the turbine operated heating compressors which heated water to a boil (a fairly low temperature at these altitudes) and pumped it to the observatory. The trough disappeared beneath the sill of the window.

A perfectly ordinary doorway was set between two of the large windows. Now the door swung open and a heavily clothed figure stepped inside. Even though Doomsday born, the fellow swayed drunkenly, as he gasped at the enriched air. Then he set down his tools and shut the door. Exterior maintenance was one of the most demanding jobs at the observatory.

A slow fan created a faint breeze in the room. The most critical problem here was to provide adequate exhaust of dead air and still keep the "perfume of life" properly concentrated. Thus the interior of the observatory was not partitioned into rooms. The entire dome was visible at a glance.

The observatory had none of the ornamentation that characterized O'rmouth, where there were laymen to be impressed. Here, everything was business. The floor was divided into sectors. Several sectors were empty—they were for the newly arrived equipment. But other sectors were piled high with supplies, oxygen containers, and astronomical equipment—much of the last quite unidentifiable. And at the center of the circular floor stood the object of all this Doomsday effort—the High Eye itself.

The Eye was the largest in the world. Even if it hadn't been stationed at the top of the world it would have stimulated awe in any astronomer. The sixty-inch mirror was hidden in plastic and ceramic structural webbing. And that spidery framework extended fifty feet into the air to support the secondary mirror—which was huge in its own right. This mirror reflected incoming light back slantwise to picturemaking machines set next to the huge mirror. The entire structure, weighing many tons, could be turned to follow any point in the sky. It was claimed that twenty-five thousand ounces of iron had gone into the steel for the bearings that made such precision possible. In the bright sunlight every detail of the structure was visible. At the same time, it was so complicated that no superstitious ornamentation was necessary to make it seem magical.

For a few moments Svir was absorbed by what many

astronomers would have given a year of their lives to investigate. Then his memories returned. He heard the sharp, tense words Tatja spoke. She stood ten feet from the wall, and faced the hallway. Her crossbow was aimed at the entrance. Six feet from her, Jolle stood, facing away from her so that he covered the astronomers who had opened the doorway.

Tatja was saying, "Move into the room slowly. Set down your equipment and line up against the wall."

From the tunnel came a puzzled question. It was Haarm Wechsler. "You refer to the Doomsday porters, of course."

Tatja replied, "I mean everyone. We suspect a saboteur is in the party and we intend to find him." Jolle turned to face directly into the tunnel. Plainly, he was more concerned about what might come out of that tunnel than with the sullen Doomsday astronomers. Svir brought his weapon to his shoulder and flicked off the safety. Now he would have a chance to show Jolle the Servant who had aroused his suspicions.

Crown's Men and Celestial Servants stumbled forward into the reddening light. Most people were too tired to care what was happening. They were coming through too fast. Tatja told them to come through in single file, but it was impossible to obey since some of the carts were drawn by two or three men, and people inevitably walked in clusters behind the oxygen wagons.

The carts were parked in a ragged formation. Then the travelers stood against the wall in a single rank. The astronomers remained at the center of the room, and their self-righteous anger was transformed into puzzlement. Why were both Crown's Men and Servants treated with equal severity? Everyone was beginning to realize that he was involved in something much more complicated than a fickle queen's whimsy.

Now every face was visible. Nowhere did Svir see that friendly, wrinkled face he had glimpsed in the dimness of the snow tunnel. Tatja glanced at Jolle, and the alien shook his head slightly.

"I don't think so," he said quietly. Then louder, to the astronomers by the telescope, "Where does that staircase lead?" He gestured with the bow at the dark hole that stood close by the hallway entrance. Svir hadn't noticed it before. It had probably been hidden from Jolle's view when the party came through in front of it.

"Living quarters, may it please Your Most Illustrious Lordship."

The sarcasm appeared to go by Jolle. "Is there any way from those quarters to the outside?"

"No. There's only that entrance, and the one by the number-three perfume dissipater." Jolle stared at the fellow for several seconds. It seemed to Svir that the alien was considering whether to go into the rock basement and search out Profirio. It would decide things once and for all, but Profirio might be planning some special ambush. Since he was trapped down there, it was probably best to leave him.

Jolle glanced at Tatja, and she said opaquely, "No, that would be—wrong." She turned back to the crowd of Crown's Men and Celestial Servants. She gestured at the stairway with her crossbow. "It is my command that you remove yourselves below. Take two extra oxygen tanks."

The Servants shuffled toward the dark stone stairs. Several of the Crown's generals stood their ground, and Minister Wechsler voiced their feelings. "Marget, you overstep the bounds of your sovereignty. The Crown's subjects deserve—your confidence. Your liaison with this fellow"—he waved at Jolle—"is most—"

"Haarm, you're in a bind you don't even know about. Get below or I'll smash you into three pieces." The Crown's officers motioned their men toward the stairs. In three minutes they were all below. Tatja walked to the hole and shut the trap. She rolled one of the supply carts over the door. It was still possible to open the trap from below, but it could not be done with stealth. She did the same at the other stairway, then walked slowly around the periphery of the dome.

Jolle said, "We want you to do two things here tonight, Svir. Be prepared to shoot any *saboteur.*" He accented the word so that Svir knew he meant one particular saboteur. "And second, help these people assemble this equipment." He waved at the carts full of picturemaking and analysis equipment.

The second job occupied Svir's time for the next four

hours. Even though Jolle and Tatja did most of the supervision, and even though the astronomers knew their equipment much better than he, he found there was much left for him to do. The Doomsday picturemakers required large quantities of mixed reagents. And much of their optical equipment was both delicate and bulky. In the end he was taking instructions from the Doomsdaymen rather than the reverse. The work was technical, and soon everyone seemed to forget that the astronomers here were working under duress. Occasionally, though, the astronomers' eyes strayed to the crossbow slung over Svir's shoulder. If they ever saw a way of tricking the gunmen below, they would not hesitate to disarm him and try to outshoot the others. The priests were, after all, being forced to reveal religious secrets they had sworn to guard forever. Fortunately, only Jolle and Tatja knew the signal which would delay the destruction deadline, and even if the priests disarmed Svir, they would have a very unpleasant surprise when they discovered how fast and dangerous the other two were.

The sun set, the snows beyond went from yellow to orange to red, and the red became deeper and deeper. Svir remembered seeing that red in the mountains from many miles away, far down in the Picchiu River so many days ago when there was still some reason, beyond revenge, for living. The thought almost drove him out of the real world. Then the stars were out. This side of the world always showed a sky much clearer and darker than beneath the sky of Seraph, where even when in crescent, the sister planet dimmed the fainter stars to invisibility. But here, thirty thousand feet above the sea and the mists, the stars were still brighter. They were so bright that the snows glittered faintly beneath their brilliance.

The wind turbine was shut off. The observatory's reservoirs now held enough hot water to support operations through the night. Besides, the hot water caused convection currents which could blur the pictures the telescope was to make. The Eye's lid was pulled back, and the perfume of life was dissipated faster to keep up with the new leak.

Then Jolle detailed his project. He gave the astronomers an area two degrees by thirty degrees and specified a search pattern. He was looking for new objects of magnitude fifteen. His instructions showed the same grasp of detail as Tatja's military plans and this in spite of the fact that he had never seen these instruments before. He knew the inclination of his boat's orbit and its distance. He probably knew the eccentricity of the orbit and initial position equally well, but he and Profirio had depended on the navigation equipment which had been destroyed by their conflict, to remember the exact position of the craft. So even though he might know the eccentricity of orbit to two digits, this wasn't good enough—he had expected to use a machine to get four or five digits. Three quarters after being marooned, he only knew the position within certain confidence limits, and this determined the area they would investigate. Fortunately, the entire search area was in the night sky at this time of year. They would take hundreds of pictures and compare them with ones that the Doomsdaymen had taken of the area in the past. At fifteenth magnitude, the vehicle must be extremely small or of low albedo.

The Doomsdaymen moved surely in the starlit dome. This was one advantage of having a fanatic regard for one's calling. They knew exactly where every piece of equipment was housed.

Doomsdaymen made their pictures on a chemical veneer set on glass plates. In order to apply this veneer evenly, they needed light—and they used a source quite mysterious to Svir. The lamp was housed in a massive pillar that was warm to the touch. Light came from a flat surface canted down from the side. It was reddish. The Doomsdaymen had discovered compounds that glowed when differentially heated. It was far better than torchlight in this oxygen-starved environment.

Finally, the first plate was inserted in the picturemaker beside the mirror. The clockwork in the base of the instrument was wound, the tube was aimed, and the exposure began It would take nearly half an hour for the plate to collect enough light to reveal objects of the sixteenth magnitude. Here was the prime advantage of the Doomsday technique over the greentint pictures used on the Tarulle Barge. Time exposures were nearly impossible with greentint.

After the first exposure, plates were changed and the telescope was repositioned. It took twenty minutes to treat the plate so that a picture was visible. Time passed and there was little for the three outsiders to do. The Doomsdaymen had spent years training for just this sort of search.

When the plates had been treated with appropriate reagents, they were placed on a glass-topped table, one of the pieces brought up with Tatja's party. The table was set above a thermoluminescent lamp. A picture taken several months earlier was set beside the new picture on the glass surface. They were positioned beneath a double eyepiece. A Doomsday astronomer carefully examined the plates. In Crownesse, this sort of equipment did not exist, since greentint astronomical pictures were of such poor quality. One eyepiece gave the operator a magnified view of a portion of one plate, and the other eyepiece did the same with the other plate. In this way, small differences could be detected between the two pictures. Even though he was standing several feet from the table, Svir could see the dim red light shining through the plates. He recognized the left-wing region of the Bat constellation captured in greater detail than he had ever seen with the thirty-inch mirror at Krirsarque. For a moment he wished he had been born in Doomsday, where all national wealth was concentrated on producing these wonderful instruments.

The hours passed slowly. There was the dull routine of setting plates, aiming the Eye, treating exposed plates, and comparing them with previous pictures. Jolle, Svir, and Tatja took positions equally spaced about the perimeter of the dome. The high windows covered so much of the walls that any intruder would set himself in silhouette unless he crawled along the floor.

It was nearly midnight when the man on the comparator called to Svir, "New object." Svir leaned over the eyepieces and looked down. The presentation was in monochrome red and black—with the black representing white, and red, darkness.. Then he realized that he was viewing a relatively indistinguished field with no stars brighter than the fourth magnitude. There was a low whirring by his ear as the Doomsdayman turned a crank on the stand. Abruptly a faint dark streak began blinking. A serrated disk rotated by the crank blanked out first the right picture and then the left.

He looked up to call Jolle, and found the other standing beside him. The alien bent over, and studied the scene for several seconds. Then with the ease of one trained on the instrument, he reached into the stem and flipped a reticle into the optics.

"That's it all right. The streak is five feet thirty inches long. That's the amount of drift it would show." Now there was the barest hint of triumph in his voice. "No more pictures, Observers. We found what we came for."

"Then you will leave us now?" came the voice of one of the more recalcitrant priests.

"Not quite yet. We will commit one more small desecration. Set the Eye on the coordinates of plate thirty-two-sixty. We must work fast since that area sets soon. It may be too hazy already. Help me will you, Svir?"

They walked to one of the carts. Jolle explained in a quieter voice, "I'm going to use the 'golem' you saw to operate my signaler. The message is complex, and my signaler has only enough power for a three-second burst." Svir remembered that military signalers had enough fuel for many hours of operation. Jolle's machine must be powerful. "That's why I needed this search," he went on. "The search area was sixty square degrees, my signaler has a dispersion of less than a degree, and the message will take nearly half a second." Behind them, Tatja herded the Doomsdaymen to one side of the room. Their help was not necessary now that the scope was tracking the required point. Now just three people were involved. Any intruder would be Profirio. For once there would be no trouble in penetrating others' disguises and ruses. Everything was very simple.

Jolle lifted the "golem" box from the cart and handed it to Svir. It was large and heavy. "Just take it over to the base of the Eye." Jolle reached into the cart and retrieved a small oblong box. By the reddish light of the comparator, its dark sides gleamed metallically.

Svir gingerly set the hand-carved cabinet on the floor beneath the picturetaking stand. The telescope moved infinitesimally just above his head. Its girders and struts stretched some fifty feet away. Beyond them hung the stars. Jolle opened the top of the cabinet. The machine's blue and green jewels glowed with painful intensity. The shifting glitter sent grotesque shadows rippling across the walls of the observatory.

There was a collective gasp from the Doomsday astronomers, then an even more impressive silence. They had thought they were dealing with madmen. But suddenly the situation was something beyond their knowledge and understanding.

Jolle reached into the shimmering heap of jewels, withdrew a metallic cable, attached it to the oblong box, and clamped the box to a telescope-alignment strut. Evidently this small box was the signaler. In the blue light his dark face held a new intensity. He sighted along the strut. "Damn. They didn't set it tracking properly." He slung his crossbow, turned to the tracking scope, and adjusted the sighting wheels. "I could use the machine in my cabinet to do the aiming, but the scope is ready-made for that sort of—"

If Svir had not been looking directly into the maze of supporting struts around the mirror, the following events would have seemed magic. In one flashing motion Profirio swung out of the scope, landed on his feet, kicked over the cabinet so that its contents fell lumpishly on the floor, and said, "Jolle killed her!" Jolle had his crossbow off his shoulder. Svir's weapon was pointed directly at Profirio's middle—killing him was merely a matter of tightening a finger. But the other's words had stopped him for nearly a half second; then Tatja had screamed from her position near the wall, "Don't, Svir!"

Then time slowed to a human pace. In a single second Profirio had forced a stalemate. Svir realized this as he glanced at Jolle, who had his weapon nearly unslung and could probably aim and fire in a tenth of a second or less. But he didn't move. Svir looked at Profirio, but he was apparently unarmed. In the wavering blue light he recognized the Celestial Servant who had talked with him in the tunnel. But now his face seemed younger. Profirio looked quite different from Jolle. Above his beard, Jolle's face was smooth, deeply tanned. But Profirio's face was paler, and deeply creased with both frown and smile lines.

Why didn't Jolle shoot? Svir glanced at Tatja. Her

crossbow was leveled and aimed—at Jolle, not Profirio. He looked at the pile of glowing jewels and saw that in the instant that Profirio accused Jolle of killing Cor, on a different level he had convinced Tatja that things were not as they seemed. Now that it lay exposed on the floor, Svir could see that Jolle's "machine" was a conglomerate of glowing crystal, which in the shifting reflections appeared transparent. A shape was imbedded in the fiery matrix. The shape was familiar. At the center was a lumpy circle some six inches across. From the lump a thick, ropelike strand extended in a rough circle. At regular intervals, finer strands split away from this main fiber—much in the way that roots furcate. Barely visible, the finest strands touched the silvery boxes that surrounded the pile.

Then he knew what had stopped Tatja in the instant it would have taken her to kill Profirio. How many times had he passed that exhibit in the anatomy section of the Krirsarque University Museum, and shuddered at the pickled brain and spinal column that hung there in a jar of preservative. Though here the spinal column was bent into a circle to conserve space, it was obvious that the general form was the same.

As it rested on the floor, the pulsating treasure whimpered. Broken away from its machine tasks and left for a moment without a program, its high-pitched voice keened over and over, "Where am I, where am I, am I . . ." and the answer was *nowhere anymore*. Several of the astronomers had fled outside, preferring anoxia to the nightmare that was developing in their shrine.

So Jolle was the slaver, after all. The revelation had strangely small effect on Svir. It was irrelevant what the dark-faced fellow had done to strangers. The barrel of his crossbow, which had drifted from Profirio toward Jolle, now swung back to the first man. The delicate stalemate that Profirio had established would soon be upset.

Svir's universe shrank to Profirio's blue-lit face, a face which would soon be destroyed. Less than five seconds had passed since the other's appearance. Now he spoke for the second time. "And this is how he did it." His hand whipped out to slap the side of the signaler. The face that hung before Svir's eyes vanished in the glare of red lightning. Even at ten feet, the heat of that beam scorched his face, just as it had once before. The beam clipped the dome, and where it touched, an explosion ripped out four square yards of the wall. Shards of wood and stone and glass fell to the floor. Prompted by this cue, the thing on the floor spoke. Its voice moved down the scale nearly an octave, *"Ter äshe gaul, Jolle."*

The memory of the last time Svir saw that light—just forty hours before—was for a moment very sharp: Jolle had maneuvered him and Cor to stand where they did. He had dismissed the signalman just before it happened. It would have been so easy to put the golem in the base of the tree and to direct it to aim the signaler that was a weapon. Svir felt his muscles jerk. All men had been puppets to these three, and now he felt himself being maneuvered as directly and unsubtly as a hunting skoat. But that didn't matter. In this moment he could remember only that charred stump—he would never quite be able to remember what Cor's face had really been like. The barrel of his crossbow swung back toward Jolle. But the bearded one hardly seemed to notice him. He was talking low and fast, to Tatja behind him. "Yes," he said, "but things are different. You love—"

Svir's finger depressed the trigger. Jolle reacted with characteristic speed, bringing his weapon down faster than Svir could even fire his weapon. Then the alien's left leg was blown off as Tatja fired. The last thing Svir felt was the explosion as Jolle's bolt smashed everything into darkness.

CHAPTER 20

The daybat fluttered down through the intricately wound branches of the needle tree, settled beside a large pink flower, and folded back its blue and orange wings. Its tiny, sleek head moved back and forth as it wiggled between the petals and licked at the juices in the base of the flower. This far from human settlement, most animals were not shy of humans—the flower under consideration was barely fifteen inches from where Svir sat.

O'rmouth was one hundred miles away. The mountains dominated the horizon to the east—if one chose to look through the leaves and green branches in that direction. Here the air was thick and rich, just warm enough so that the breeze moving along the ground was pleasantly cool. Here the sunlight was muted by green leaves, not reflected back with merciless intensity by snow and ice.

Three hundred feet away, their battle group was setting up bivouac. The universe had chosen to wear its mask of light and love today. Svir recognized the deception. The real world was snow and ice and red thunderbolts that . . .

There was a swishing and a crackling as Tatja entered the little open spot by the tent and sat down beside him. The daybat jerked its head from the flower and looked warily about, then went back within the bedraggled pink mass.

They sat in silence for several minutes. Tatja wore a gray fatigue uniform. There was about her none of the purpose or intensity that had driven her before. The

Doomsdaymen were far behind them. There were no more threats to face.

Tatja's arm slipped onto his elbow. Then her face was before his and her eyes bore the same quiet, personal interest that he had seen more than four years ago in a certain tavern in Krirsarque—where this dream had begun. "I'm sorry, Svir. I don't really know that I should feel more unhappy about you than about all the other people who were killed in this adventure. I guess I just know you too well . . . and that makes your situation more important to me. If there's anything I can do to . . ."

He tried to produce an ironic chuckle but all that came out was a croaking sound.

"What?" asked Tatja.

He opened his mouth again and spoke. The words came fast, low, slurred. "I was just thinking that if Jolle's golem had been a bit more accurate, you would be making the same offer to Cor now."

She raised her hand to his shoulder. "I think I might, Svir. She did much for both of us. But the golem was perfectly accurate. Jolle had no intention of killing you—you knew astronomy. He wanted you as a technician and as a trustworthy servant. By killing her, he changed a persistent nuisance into—he thought—an ally even more faithful than I. It was only bad luck that Jolle's plan did not work. You see, Profirio was within one hundred yards of the bunker when the golem fired the signaler. Pröfe had already been separated from his supporters. He was trying to move across the no-man's-land to our side. He saw the murder—at least he saw the golem. Eventually he learned who had been killed. He talked to you during the walk up the snow tunnel. By the time we had reached the observatory, he knew how Jolle was using you, and he knew how to approach you.

"He did sneak below the main floor, as we thought. But you remember that the hot water from the wind turbines had to go into those quarters. The pipe was too small for him, but the earth around the entrance hole was not rocky. Pröfe dug his way out during the first hours. Jolle was too near his goal to take everything into account and I . . . I haven't been very much of an analyst ever since . . .

Anyway, Pröfe got outside, and while you and Jolle were mounting the signaler, he crawled onto the dome and down into the telescope."

Svir's attention wandered. His eyes moved past her face, back to the bat on the branch above them. The flower juices splashed over the lip of the petals and a sweet smell drifted down upon them. He had no interest in what had happened in the last hundred hours—whether the world had been saved or not. His hands clenched and unclenched as he considered what he would do if that bat were so incautious as to move around to the bottom of the branch.

Tatja saw this. Her hand moved across his shoulder and she moved closer. "Svir, you weren't the only one who had his world kicked to pieces. I loved Jolle. I suppose it shows that intelligence has little control over sex. Certainly if I hadn't fallen, none of the rest would have happened. Cor would be alive.

"But this doesn't change that fact that I really loved him. Jolle turned out to be evil, but he was also a . . . someone stronger than I, who made a great show of liking me. Pröfe is a kinder man. But he's not Jolle.

"I'm going to disappear tonight. So is Pröfe. I won't go into the details—I'm afraid they wouldn't be completely intelligible—but Pröfe signaled their vehicle last night, and we have transportation now. I imagine Haarm Wechsler will be quite relieved. The Bureaucrats will have to find a Crown Surrogate, but after the way I treated them above O'rmouth, I don't think they're interested in having a ruler as unreliable as I. They may even believe I'm something supernatural.

"There's so much I must learn. Enough to fill thousands of years. Jolle and Pröfe have both explained many things to me, but I know my education has not yet begun." For a moment there was excitement in her voice. "And everyone I meet will be like me. Svir, my situation is the same as yours—and I can see great happiness in it. Don't you?"

The bat undid its wings and fluttered to the next flower—ten inches from the first. It was still not more than fifteen inches from his head.

Tatja tried a different track. "Svir, you are going to live through the first stages of the most exciting period of Tu's history. In the next two hundred years, the people of Tu will move science along to the beginnings of what you have seen with Jolle and Pröfe. No slavers will deny you progress. In three centuries human nature itself will change, and all that went before will be chrysalis. Your five-times great grandchildren will be like me.

"But you will never see me or Pröfe. . . . I guess you're just as happy about that." The bat turned, and one wing draped down so low that Svir could see the individual blue and orange hairs that composed its fur. "But," Tatja continued, hoping somehow to get through to him, "we or people like us will never be far away. There are many wrong turnings that the unguided can take. There are pestilences that could kill all life on the planet—if you misuse the discoveries you will make. We will try to protect you—in appropriate, undetectable ways."

Svir's clenched hands became claws as they flashed up. Tatja caught his wrists in the first four inches of motion. Her grip was unshakable. And for once she misunderstood his motives. "Please, Svir. I don't mean protection like you've been receiving in the last ten days. People were killed and ruined here because we were fighting a superman, not someone who could be easily outmaneuvered. Never again will we start wars in order to prevent greater catastrophe. I hadn't realized how twisted this has left you. You got caught right in the middle, as I did; but I was their equal—and you were nearly destroyed. If Pröfe had any equipment with him, he could cure you, make you realize that there are still ways out.

"I take back what I said before: I will return. Soon. The cure is simple, and I owe you more than that. . . ." She let his hands fall back into his lap, and for a moment her lips brushed his cheek. She stood up slowly, and left the clearing. For several minutes he could hear her moving through the brush toward the nearest camping area.

His eyes never left the beautiful mammal that moved so delicately on the branch. It had moved on top of the branch, but now it was edging back under. Its clear black eyes gazed down at him. In a moment . . .

Svir lunged up to catch the bat in a two-handed crushing blow. But the little animal was too fast, and it flashed from between the approaching hands. It fluttered up through the branches and into the blue spaces above.